MW00915521

The Ashen Yard

Jeff Spaur

First off, thank you to my wife for being gracefully patient with me in this process. A continued extension to my sons, both who are so excited their father wrote a book.

A huge shout-out to all my readers, in particular Rachel, Amy, Kristin, and Robin, who provided valuable feedback and encouragement.

To Chiara for her incredible cover artwork.

To my editor, Michaela, for helping me clean this story up, delivering her insight and perspective, and providing words of encouragement that helped me cross the finish line.

Lastly to the reader, thank you for giving this a chance. I hope you enjoy the experience.

- Chapter 1 -

I'm not ready to take another life. This is my reality.

My hand flies across the canvas strengthening the bold lines. Art is the therapy that helps me cope. The gentle shades add layers of depth to help define the shadows. My hand drops as I analyze my work. What's on the canvas isn't my usual style. A large tree uprooted by a gale force wind. Another sign? God, I hope not.

Taking another life. It's coming. I want control but know I'm bound. I shiver before rising from the grassy nook under the tree.

The sun's light reminds me of the time. The medical dispensary opened about twenty minutes ago. Time to complete my errand before heading to the Forum.

I glance down at my payment card. The digital fifty sits at the top, just enough. A year ago, my mother caught an illness she hasn't been able to recover from. I'm hoping, as I always do, that this new prescription will improve her health. We don't need another looming threat hovering over our miserable lives.

It's difficult to keep track of how many times her medication has changed. I swear it's a new prescription with every medical evaluation. In the beginning, the medicines cost ten credits, but the price keeps increasing. Fortunately, I sold a drawing yesterday. Any extra income helps.

As I walk, my eyes trace the massive titanium wall that sits about two hundred feet away. These walls keep us inside. This is where they say we belong.

Someone's using the medical dispensary, which sticks out of the wall like a sore.

My feet scuff the dirt. The noise startles the guy using the dispensary. He twitches and looks over his shoulder. We make eye contact and his eyes widen. I recognize him from school. We were sparring partners one time, and I rattled him good. He couldn't land a single hit. Everyone knew how unfair it was for Vincent to partner us up. I pulled back enough not to completely wreck him.

"I'm sorry," his voice shakes. "I just finished." He returns his attention to the screen, presses one more time, and steps to the side. "All done."

I nod. He stands there, frozen. "Are you going to move so I can use it?" I ask.

He stutters. "Oh, right. See you." He runs off, trips over a tree root, and falls. Embarrassed, he jumps up, dusts off, and continues running.

At the dispensary, I scan my identification card. The screen requests my prints and I place my hand upon the screen. The computer flashes with my identity proven. Another screen follows with a *confirmed* message.

A pleasant voice pushes through the dispensary console, "Good morning Brock. How may I assist you today?"

"Just another prescription." I punch in the number.

"Give me one second while I process your request." Within a moment, a number scrolls across the screen. "Will you please verify the prescription number?"

My eyes scan the number. "That's the one."

"Looks like there's an update on this prescription." She clears her throat. "I need to inform you the payment for this medicine increased to 100 credits."

I choke before finding my voice. "Are you kidding?" Even though I know the answer, I glance at my payment card where digital fifty mocks me. Teeth clenched, I punch the dispensary. "I can't believe this." A vision plays showing my mother lying in bed coughing. "You're already robbing me blind." Another hit, and this time the image blurs.

The female voice comes out patient and calm. "I'm truly sorry. You know I have nothing to do with the prices." A pause. "Off the record, if I made the decisions, I'd give you what you needed."

Another pause.

"Is this for your mom again?" she asks.

Dammit. Why did I share personal details with this voice? Is her voice lovely? Yes. Does she appear to show compassion? Yes. But this won't help my mother.

"It's not your business." Guilt courses through my veins for being curt.

Even through the speaker, I hear the quiver in the response, "Of, of course not."

"No matter." A shred of hope crosses my mind. "I'll try my luck in the Forum. Hopefully, I can sell some drawings today."

"Good luck."

"Yeah," I say, hitting the sign off button. I punch the screen again before leaving.

My black duffel bag rests on my shoulder. I walk toward the Forum, kicking the dirt path along the way. The evergreen trees spread around the area like a child's blanket, comforting. This feeling reminds me of my mother. She needs that medicine. Whoever is responsible for their greed is going to pay. Desperation falters my confidence. I'm powerless.

Others wait at the Forum's entrance. I detour to a decrepit building that looks like a sad dog in the middle of a rainstorm. This is the Locker Room.

Inside, the man at the counter nods. Even though we interact regularly, we barely make conversation. This fits the culture within the Ashen Yard.

"Locker three," his gruff voice croaks under his giant brown beard. He hands me a lock and key and promptly returns to using his knife to pick under his fingernails.

Locker three it is. I unsnap my utility belt from my waist, set my belt along with my two handguns in the locker. Weapons are prohibited inside the Forum.

Reaching into my bag, I pull out a different set of clothes. Time to change from the simple black shirt and faded blue jeans to the dull prison garb: shirt and pants with an alternating dark gray, light gray pattern. Everything dull, everything gray. Patched on the back of the shirt is my number in large print, #54578.

I snap the lock closed.

My duffel bag draws upon my hope. Not many items are allowed in the Forum, but drawings are one of them. I'm outside and stand near the door looming like a giant mouth. Here's the glorious exit of the prison.

- Chapter 2 -

My eyes circle around the mishmash of people. Everyone is young, no one over the age of twenty. Someone whistles, a sign of discomfort, a sign of weakness. The enormous door lifts open breaking the awkward moment. One by one people exit from the chamber and move toward the Locker Room. Eye contact with the ground is popular. Everyone looks defeated.

The scanner flashes green, signaling everyone waiting to proceed into the tunnel. The entrance scans us to ensure nothing dangerous enters. The light stays green as everyone steps inside. We cleared the first security step.

My eyes squint, adjusting to the fluorescent lights. The giant door slides closed behind us. A smaller door on the opposing side opens. The next clearance step allows one person at a time. We gladly wait to escape this life for a few small moments.

I walk through the door where armed guards await the prisoners. They stand by three doors holding manual scanners, one extra precaution.

A guard signals me over and says, “Identification please.” Not a single inch of his skin shows. His darkened visor hides his face. Even though I cannot read his facial expressions, the disgust threading his voice is enough to tell how he feels about a criminal like me.

There are days I like to mess with them. However, today is not a day to be denied the Forum. I'll play nice.

He uses a handheld to scan the bottom of my ID. It blinks green. "Feet and legs shoulder width apart and arms parallel to the ground."

I abide his command. He scans my body before patting me down. I want to be a smartass and ask him if he enjoys feeling me up, but I bite my tongue. He finishes his search and continues the same routine with my bag.

"Access granted," the guard says. He sounds disappointed. They enjoy sending us back to our hellhole.

Stepping through, I'm greeted by the Forum. This place is the neutral barrier that divides the Ashen Yard from the Acropolis. It's here that criminals and law-abiding citizens, or Pawns as we call them, conduct business. Inside the Forum is an industrial park and a marketplace filled with various vendors.

One might wonder why criminals are allowed to interact with Pawns. The main reason is our craftsmanship and cheap labor. Some, like myself, freelance our goods. Others are hired by companies to make quality goods for little pay.

While Pawns enter the Forum at their own risk, there's a large amount of protection in place. Guards patrol the market, skilled marksmen have an aerial view from thirty-foot towers, and surveillance cameras cover every nook and cranny. Each guard is connected to a headset, molding them into a cohesive unit.

For criminals, access to the Forum is like work release. Being able to work and barter inside a social marketplace is a glorious recess, one we don't want to forfeit. But the freedom is also a reminder of the prison in which we reside.

As I walk toward my usual booth in the art section, I filter through streams of people and hear the familiar sounds of business. Hundreds of voices fill the air with an array of conversations. From the factories comes the thunderous sounds of large machinery, singing the tune of the day's orders. The industrial park of the Forum smells like sweat and feels like determination.

My wooden vendor stand is located at the end of a row, I pull out my drawings and set them on display. In the art section, a rainbow of colors flood the eyes. That's where I stand out. My art is shades of gray. I do this for two reasons. First, color costs money. Second, gray represents my life story.

I wait for customers. Polite greetings and farewells bathe my ears, but nobody approaches my booth. My fingers tap. Someone needs to buy. I imagine my mother exhausted and lying in bed.

As if my frustration were transmitted through the air, my most regular customer approaches the booth. I run my hand down the front of my shirt to spread out the wrinkles. My attempt fails.

"Good afternoon, Mr. P," I say. Mr. P is a man in his late-thirties who's showing signs of early gray. We nearly stand eye to eye. He stands an inch shorter than me at six feet. He's always dressed in an expensive black business suit with a perfectly straight tie. Today's tie happens to be a pattern of red with black diagonal lines.

He greets me with a warm smile. "Good afternoon." He courteously bows his head. "Do you have anything new today?"

"I only have one new piece." My voice comes out rushed. Not the way I want to begin a sale.

I point to the drawing I completed this morning. "I wish I had time to craft some more, but things are getting busy."

"Busy," he repeats with a half snort. "It's sort of scary to think of what you mean by that word."

My gaze grows cold. The fact my life amuses him rubs me

the wrong way. He simply has no idea.

"You know," he says to break the awkward exchange. "You look like someone I used to know." He rubs the stubble under his chin. "I own a number of your pieces and I don't know your name. The BA in the bottom right corner of your drawings I assume are your initials."

His comment catches me off guard. Pawns don't take the time to care about criminals. Mr. P is my most regular customer. Our conversations are amiable and businesslike. There's no need to know each other's names. "No offense sir, does it really matter?"

He pauses and rubs his chin again. "I guess you're right. It doesn't." A chuckle escapes his mouth. "Well, I like the new drawing. I'll take it. The usual price?"

"Actually," I begin as my thoughts shift to my mother. "It's fifty today."

He looks at me like I asked him to pay with a finger. "That's double the price!"

A lump forms in my throat. I'm taking a risk. I need to play this right. "Consider the increased price as charity. It's for medicine, and the medicine is not for me."

I attempt to read his reaction. He flinches. "I'll pay only if you tell me who it's for."

Dammit. Why didn't I say it was for me? I made this mistake already with her – the voice. What the hell, no point in lying. I swallow my reservations, "It's for my mother."

Mr. P huffs and his eyebrows raise with intrigue. "Your mother lives in there with you? What, are you a family of criminals?"

The question pisses me off. My right hand trembles. It wants to fight. Instead of answering his question, my eyes glare. "Are you going to buy or not?" Maybe too much heat.

Holding up his hands, he replies, "I'm sorry, that came out wrong. And yes, of course I'll pay."

Our payment cards connect. He punches in fifty credits to

transfer. Transaction confirmed. In a split second, my payment card digitally reads one hundred.

Mr. P takes the drawing off its stand and looks at me. “Again, I apologize.” He waits for my response, but it doesn’t come. He takes another look at the drawing before giving a small wave and walking off.

I look at the time, three-thirty. I continue to stay open to make a bit of extra money. I would like to bring some fresh food home. Luck shows its face when another customer stops by and purchases a drawing. I don’t press my luck and sell it for twenty-five credits.

I pack up and aim for the food vendors. Twenty-five credits isn’t much, but I grab enough fresh produce to make a modest salad.

The transaction just finishes when a large groaning noise comes from one of the factories followed by an impact that vibrates the ground. Cries and screams echo from the factory.

- Chapter 3 -

A crowd gathers. Panicked cries like, "Where's my son?" and "My husband works in there!" travel through the air.

The guards order everyone back. Little red dots swivel around the crowd from the marksmen in the towers. The guards remain on high alert because chaos creates distractions. Criminals like distractions.

After a couple of minutes, a few men are carried out of the factory. The one who looks the worst is like me, a criminal, with both legs bent in unnatural positions. The sight sickens me because he will receive crude medical treatment, never be able to work again, and then looked upon as an animal ready to be put down. He'll last one day after being released. The harsh truth of the Ashen Yard.

As the excitement settles, the electrifying sound of sirens burst out. Heads spin around in confusion. I look toward the guard towers. I follow the direction the marksmen turn, toward the entrance of the Acropolis, the place I've never been. A guard fires at a man dressed in the same garb as me who is just feet from the entrance. The bullet penetrates his back. The man falls into a lifeless heap on the ground.

People shout and run in all directions. My mind is alert. Another shot fires and full-on panic ensues.

My eyes connect with a criminal about ten feet in front of me sneaking his hand into a Pawn's purse.

It never fails. With agile movements, I close the gap. He's about to slip into the crowd, but I grab his wrist. I twist his arm behind him until it feels like the tendons in his shoulder will tear. He lets out a sharp cry. I punch his face and a tooth flies from his mouth and he falls unconscious.

I scoop the wallet from the ground and meet the eyes of the woman. Without saying a word, I hand it to her. As the exchange happens, a blow hits my back, and I fall face first. My body nearly crushes the bag of food and my duffle bags lands in front of me.

"You keep your hands off her, criminal," comes a gruff voice.

With a wince, I twist around to see a guard standing a few feet away. The butt of his gun points in my direction.

The woman walks over to my bag and brings it to me. "It's okay, he actually fought to get this back for me."

The doubt in his voice is thick. "A low-life piece of crap like this?"

She nods.

I roll onto my back and face the two of them. "Is this how you reward good citizenship?" My hand massages the stinging pain.

The guard raises his face plate. He looks much older than I anticipated. Disgust flares from his eyes. "There isn't anything good about low life scum like you. Now turn over so I don't have to look at your ugly mug." He spits in my direction and points his gun with an audible click.

I make friends with the ground. If we were on level ground, I'd take him out before he could blink. But we are not on level ground, and this is my current playing field.

In this moment, I realize my exit out of the Forum will take a long time. First the Pawns will receive a secure exit, and then the criminals will be herded like dogs. This means the dispensary will close before I get out of here. I pound my fist on the ground. All I can do is wait.

- Chapter 4 -

The guards handle the evacuation. Before long, the criminals are herded back like sheep. Our belongings aren't checked as closely when we go back into the Ashen Yard. There are no Pawns to hurt there. It's just a quick scan for stolen goods.

I don't waste time. My feet move to the Locker Room. I gather my stowed possessions. Conversations between criminals tread through the room.

"Why does some idiot have to ruin it for us?" says a criminal who looks about my age. His hair is so blonde it's almost white. "I mean, how far did he think he was going to get anyway?"

"Getting into the Forum is going to be more difficult now," says another, younger one. His hair is black like the dark sky.

One of them looks at me and says, "Hey, you're the one who nearly busted my arm." The wallet thief glares at me. My attention moves back to my boots.

The lack of interest hits a nerve. "What? You got nothing to say?" He stands up, arms hanging at his sides with fists clenched, muscles taut. Blood laces his mouth from his lost tooth.

I shake my head and a laugh escapes. "You shouldn't take things that aren't yours."

Three voices laugh at once. Useful information.

"Look at you all high and mighty," the thief spits. "You think you're special?" More laughs come from the group. "Nobody in this hellhole is a saint. You're no better than us."

I stand up, my eyes level with his. I wrap my utility belt around my waist. The thief's eyes shoot down when he notices the guns.

"Oh, look here fellas, we got ourselves someone who thinks he's *real* special." I grab my black shirt from the bench. He looks back at his friends. "Those clothes? Must be Quentin."

Hearing Quentin's name sets me on edge. I hiss through my teeth. "I don't bow to anyone."

"Well, you aren't fooling me."

This idiot isn't worth my time. I gather my duffel bag and food before heading to the door. Before I make it, one of them shouts, "Gentlemen's Duel." I turn around and notice for the first time how many people are inside. Uncertainty and discomfort rummage the faces.

"I'll be outside," I reply to the request.

Everyone funnels out of the Locker Room. My duffel bag rests on the ground with my utility belt. I empty anything that can be used as a weapon. A Gentlemen's Duel holds a code of conduct. The only weapon allowed is the body. Nobody breaks these rules, because even in prison, there's honor.

The onlookers gather around in a circle, forming a fighting ring. The thief and I square off face to face. The beginning of the duel opens with each criminal stating why they're in the Ashen Yard.

"What are you in for?" the thief asks. He continues to speak as though he didn't ask the question. "I'm in for grand larceny and manslaughter." He sneers.

My hand moves to my mouth as I laugh. A low murmur

cycles through the circle of spectators.

His eyes shoot daggers. "Fine big shot, what did you do?"

This time he gives me time to respond. "Being born."

Confusion traces his face. I almost see the wheels inside his brain trying to connect the dots. "What do you mean? We're all in here for a reason."

I refuse to respond, just stare.

His eyes flicker, "What are you saying? You Prisonborn or something?"

I nod my head and watch as he falters. I can't hold back the smile. Anyone born in prison who's healthy after eighteen years is tough as nails.

He turns around to look at his two friends, their eyes wide. He gives a nonchalant shrug. "You ready or what?" The shake in his voice overrides any confidence.

I hold my hands out like I've been waiting this whole time.

He charges full force and swings his fist as hard as he can.

His attack is laughable. I catch his fist with my left hand and counterpunch with my right. Blood splashes across his face, and he drops for the second time on my account. The fight is over. Everyone in the circle looks on with open mouths, speechless, motionless. The thief's friends run over and help him to his feet. He's disoriented, probably concussed.

I look at his friends. "Make sure he stays awake." They look apprehensive. "If you let him fall asleep, he may never wake up." They nod in understanding. I turn around, gather my possessions, and walk away.

Within a short distance, a voice calls for me and footsteps race my direction. I turn around to acknowledge the voice.

"You were amazing," an unfamiliar face says. His dark hair is unkempt and falls over his eyes. He's skinny like he doesn't eat enough. The blue shirt indicates he works for Valentine – my boss's rival. "How did you learn to fight so well?"

"Survival."

"I don't doubt it," he says shaking his head. He snorts, "You have a lot of confidence, don't you?"

Confidence is necessary for survival. I keep walking.

A brief pause. He runs up beside me again, walking with me now, "You do the drawings don't you? The black and whites?"

My annoyance surfaces. I don't value conversations with anyone except my mother. "Yes," I reply hoping he'll take the hint.

"I like your artistic style. Your details are meticulous, and the gray is bold. Who do you work for?"

"Look," I say as I turn to face him. "If I answer, will you quit talking to me?"

His shoulders sag. I roll my eyes. "Quentin is my Lord, as if my shirt didn't give it away."

"All right, sorry to bother you." He pauses. "It's too bad we aren't on the same side. I might like you then."

I shrug my shoulders and release eye contact with a potential enemy. "Trust me, you're not missing much. I don't do friends."

This ends our conversation. We split in our respective directions, him toward the west, and me toward the east.

- Chapter 5 -

My thoughts distract me from what's supposed to be my stroll to my apartment. Instead, I end up at the dispensary. I look at the dark console. My reflection stares back at me. Anger and anxiety stir in my stomach. It's okay. This will be my first stop in the morning.

I take another detour before I call it a night. Some solitude sounds appealing. My mother may worry, but I've never failed to return home.

Behind the blocks of apartment buildings in the residential area is a perfect, cozy spot where I nestle near three mature evergreens. Where I started the day–my drawing spot. This peaceful place is where I forget my life. This spot settles my mind and catalyzes my artistic expressions.

I enjoy drawing on nights like tonight; the soft moonlight glows through the tree branches. In the early mornings, birds perch on the branches and sing their songs. I pretend they tell me exciting events from the outside. I sit down and listen to their melody.

I pull compressed charcoal sticks out of my bag and a small canvas that's hungry for my contours. Leaning back against the trunk, I inhale. The grass feels like a seated cushion. A warm feeling engulfs me in the night's fresh air.

Stars litter the sky complimenting the half-moon. This is as peaceful as it gets here.

With a clear mind, my hand takes flight across the canvas. My drawings capture a memory, a desire, a feeling bottled up within the depths of my soul. Drawing is such a habit that my mind wanders as I work.

Welcome to the Ashen Yard. Where survival is a prerequisite. This place became a popular government program a couple of generations ago. The war on crime became a financial pit with no end in sight. With the economic crisis, it became worse. People were trying to survive. The worst came in the larger cities. Citizens cried for sanctuary. Responding to the outcry, the government worked hand in hand with criminals, and their solution became societal prisons; a large, designated piece of land where crime marks no punishment. The outer walls of the prison stand fifty feet in the air. Fortunately, the place is not a closed dome, so the sky is not hidden, fresh air swirls inside, and the occasional wildlife graces its appearance.

Each major metropolis in the United States contains a piece of land like this. Outside of the Ashen Yard is called the Acropolis where Pawns live in peace and prosperity. The agreement between the criminals and the government is simple. Commit as much crime within the prison and keep it from escaping the walls. The Lords are the supreme rulers of the prison and even though there is not direct proof, we know they receive government benefits.

Imagine the sky took a massive dump to form this place. The buildings falling apart and only shoddy patchwork keeps them standing. The only strip of beauty comes from the large green trees and collections of moss native to the Pacific Northwest, even this cannot hide the filth left by its inhabitants.

A Pawn's natural conclusion to this prison would be that it looks like chaos and anarchy, but it's a self-sustaining society.

Despite a prison, people crave structure. Codes of conduct exist.

They also imagine hard criminals who deserves this life. I'm Prisonborn, a forgotten child. I became a victim bystander of the system. The only crime I committed is entering this world.

Of course, that changed over time. I've committed more crimes than I care to admit. I don't qualify my actions as crimes, more like survival. The Ashen Yard's environment is survival of the fittest, and so far, I'm fit.

I pull away from my thoughts and focus on my canvas. My hand replicated the event in the Forum. Men carrying the injured on stretchers. The onlookers questioning the scene.

Another drawing calls my name. My hand returns to its natural work. My mind reverts to the conversation with Mr. P. It's unheard of for a Pawn to ask for the name of a criminal. Sure, they enjoy our arts and crafts, but that is the extent of the relationship. Mr. P asked for my name. It felt like a small step to feeling like an actual person.

Most Pawns have judgy eyes and label me a murderer, lowlife, scum. I wish I could tell them I don't fit their predispositions. Yes, I have killed. But am I a murderer? I mean, what would they do in a situation where killing someone meant saving yourself? They'll never understand.

I wish I responded differently. My pessimism spilled from my mouth. 'Does my name matter?' – of course it matters! Since the day I was born, all freedom and liberty were stripped from me. My identity is something they cannot take away.

Ten minutes expire before I finish. I look down at the canvas. The drawing is of a face. The face of a boy. The boy's hair is short, and his ears stick out. He looks young, but his youth fails to capture innocence. The physical features are unnaturally rough. There are no laugh lines on the face. Hatred in his eyes. Then the realization hits me. This is the face of the first life taken by my hands.

- Chapter 6 -

A bit disturbed by my drawing, I call it a night. As I approach my apartment, the calmness of night rests its head upon the worn-out building. The moon's subtle light shines proudly. The darkness shades the ugliness and tears the face of reality. This illusion generates a feeling of home. Fighting seldom happens around the residential areas, but the buildings look as though they suffer through a battle every day. Picture them crumbling with one wrong Jenga move.

Walking up the rickety staircase to my third story apartment, the grinding steps tell me a story. I reach the tiny balcony where my apartment rests. My hand reaches for the ancient rusty door and, spinning the knob, the door opens with a squeak.

Inside the apartment, everything is quiet and dark. Even rundown, the space is cozy and feels welcoming. The initial entryway to the apartment opens into a large room containing our living area, dining area, and kitchen. A small hallway runs to the end of our living room where the bathroom and two bedrooms are located.

As expected, there's no sign of my mother. She seems to tire sooner than normal. I don't blame her one bit, the illness and stress conjures fatigue. I'm grateful I can delay the bad news about her medicine.

I hang my utility belt on the shelf inside the doorway. I place my guns and bag of drawings upon the kitchen table. My bag settles next to a hand-written note.

Brock,

I'm sorry I couldn't stay up long enough to see you home. I'm so tired. You can fill me in tomorrow during breakfast. There's leftover chicken in the cold box for dinner.

Love you,

Mom

A smile forms as I put the note down. My mother always ensures my well-being. Her greatest fear is her son becoming a mindless monster within this prison. She taught me how to maintain my decency and humanity in this world.

My greatest fear matches my mother's, and there are times when it appears I may transform into a monster. The drawing of the boy enters my mind. Many monstrous moments litter my life, but I'm not a monster. I shiver and push the thought aside.

The vegetables peek out of my bag. Unraveling the supplies from the market, I prepare a fresh salad. The leftover chicken in the cold box is wrapped in plastic. The scent lifts to my nose and calls upon my hunger. The hunger consumes me. I don't hold back and make another small salad and scarf down the remainder of the chicken.

With the meal complete, I store the rest of the produce in the cold box. Before heading into the hallway, the sofa in the living room looks inviting. My mother tries to make this place look like a home. Displayed across the walls are some of my drawings, mixed with family pictures and a few other living decorations my mother had me purchase in the Forum. Dispersed around the room is a small assortment of furniture. There are a couple of end tables, a worn-out coffee table, and a TV stand with a TV that hasn't worked in who knows how long.

I relax on the sofa and lean back. My hand rubs the tiny bite marks on the arm of the sofa. This was my favorite chewing spot when I was a child. Some sort of expensive sauce spilled here. My little chewers latched on, and my mother believes I continued to chew there in hope for more of the savory taste. This story is one of her favorites to retell.

The time beckons for bed. My boots squeak along the floorboards until I reach by my mother's door. As quietly as possible, I peer in and see the subtle rise and fall of her chest.

I walk over to the side of her bed and sit down next to her. Seeing her sleep makes her look like she's actually at peace. Worry lines and strands of gray hair reveal the years of stress which make her look much older than her thirty-seven years of age. I pray she didn't worry too much. I do that enough as it is.

My weight shifts and her body makes a subtle movement. I freeze. She nestles back into the coziness of her bed. That signals my leave. She needs her rest.

My room welcomes me for the night. I turn on my bedside lamp and place my handguns on my dresser. Opening my bag, I place my drawings upon my desk. My hand bumps a small picture frame, and it flies toward the ground. My quick reflexes scoop the frame before it crashes. The frame returns to its spot on my desk, and I look at its contents. It's a picture of my mother and I when I was four years old. My mother's face is hard, but there's still youthfulness in her eyes. Strands of gray hair have yet to contaminate the blonde. And then there's me, standing without a smile as usual. She always wanted me to smile for pictures, but I always refused. As a little boy, I had a hard time finding happiness. As time progressed, not much changed, but I do try to lighten up at times because it makes her happy. She wants to know I'm alive inside. It lessens her guilt. She doesn't want me to hate her for bringing me into this godforsaken world.

I change into nighttime attire and reach underneath my

bed pulling out a small crate of books. Having books and reading is frowned upon by the Lords. The less educated they keep the criminals, the more they can maintain compliance.

I thank my mother for books. She is different. She values education. There used to be a chair in the corner of my room when I was younger. I remember my mother sitting down with me every night to read stories. She effectively planted the seed for learning, a seed that's blossomed.

Just like drawing, reading is another form of escape. I pull a book out of the crate that I'm halfway through. It's a science fiction novel about a young man who becomes a fighter pilot. Tyranny fills the limits of space, and it's his job to help combat it. The book occupies me for an hour before I turn off my light, set my alarm, and give in to the night.

It feels as though I just shut my eyes and the sound of gunshots punctuate the night. I stir from the dangerous alarm clock. It takes a moment to wipe the sleep from my eyes. It's two in the morning.

Colorful curses escape my mouth. I check the magazines of my handguns. A full fifteen rounds securely fastened inside the chambers.

Grogginess blurs my vision. Peering outside, I gather a glimpse of the commotion. Looking down three stories, two kids, no more than thirteen years old, are fighting. They are both reloading their guns behind separate piles of garbage in the streets below.

Idiots. The young ones are eager to impress the Lords.

Guns ready to fire, the curtains slide providing an opening through the rod iron bars. I fire two rounds in the direction of each kid, intentionally missing. They sprint in their respective directions like fleeing dogs.

Mumbling under my breath, I re-secure my window and shut the curtain. Time to finish my last few hours of bliss before facing reality.

Instead of returning my gun to my dresser, it rests under

my pillow. I may need them again before my real alarm goes off. I realize those two shouldn't have had guns. Guns are only distributed during battles or with certain permissions from a Lord. This odd evolution is too brain demanding this early in the morning. I ease my mind to catch a few more moments of sleep.

- Chapter 7 -

Beep, beep, beep. The alarm clock nearly falls to the ground after my slap. Now this is how I should wake up. Stretching out my arms and legs, a couple snap, crackle, pops spring relief and help me release a deep breath.

The sun's rays come through the curtains. It makes me squint. Should I open the window? No, I don't want to be too depressed before seven.

With a batch of fresh clothes, I exit my room. The floorboards groan as I walk down the hallway toward the bathroom. Today is a shower day. The light inside shines under the doorway. I step back knowing my mother is inside.

My knuckles tap the door, "You going to be long?"

"One second," my mother replies in her sweet voice. "I'm nearly done."

A few seconds pass and the door opens. My mother steps out in her tattered robe with a towel wrapped around her head. Her eyes soften. An unusual sparkle emits from her look.

"Even though all our eyes are gray, yours always seem different, more alive," she says.

"You never let me forget."

She places her hand on my shoulder. "Get cleaned up, and

I will have breakfast ready by the time you finish." She kisses me on the cheek and walks toward the kitchen.

Inside the bathroom, the cracked mirror taunts me. I splash water over my face. My fingers trace the subtle scars on my face. They scream at me, a reminder of who I am. I don't understand what my mother sees in my eyes. I only see a dull, depressing gray, as if they're void of life.

Our eyes mark our punishment. Each prisoner's melanin in the iris is drained. Our eyes are a slap in the face. They stand as a constant reminder of the dead lives we lead. This punishment is one of the greatest distinctions between a prisoner and a Pawn.

I lather my face for a shave before jumping in the shower. My face comes away with little cuts. I splash my face with more water and use a towel to staunch the blood.

My fingers move through my black hair. They pull away and look like a hiking trail.

In the shower the warm water soothes my body. I stand there for a couple extra minutes, savoring every moment because it doesn't happen every day.

I'm out and ready for the day, dressed in simple light blue jeans and a black t-shirt. I head toward the kitchen. Sitting on the table waiting for me is a stack of my mother's homemade pancakes drizzled with syrup and a few slices of bacon piled on the side. The prepared breakfast is exceptional compared to the oatmeal mush I normally eat.

"What's the special occasion?" I ask my mother. "When did we get bacon? I didn't bring any home last night."

"Oh, well you know," her words stumble. "I got a job yesterday while you were at school." Her eyes avert mine.

I look out the kitchen window. I know the answer to my question, but I ask anyway. "What kind of job?"

"Just a job." Eye contact still avoided.

My head shakes in disgust. My stomach turns like I'm going to be sick. Anytime we get something nice, she provides a service for a scumbag.

The slimy image of what she may have done for the bacon makes my chest burn. "You don't have to do this for me!"

My mother counters and slams both hands on the table. "Brock, don't tell me not to take care of you! You leave here every day, and I don't know if you'll come back." Her gray eyes shine. Tears stream down her cheeks. Her intense gaze holds directly into my own.

My eyes wander down to her hands on the table. A memory.

I remember when strange visitors came rolling into our apartment. I was six years old when I figured why. A man comes and visits. Mother asks me to keep myself busy. The man leaves. We have food we didn't have before.

Even at a young age, kids are smarter than adults give them credit for. I didn't fully understand, but I knew enough. Eventually that knowledge grew on me, and I despised what was happening. I began to resent my father for dying. Why did my mother have to suffer?

I decided to fight back when I was ten years old. A sleazy men finished his business with my mother. He walked out of the bedroom. I was sitting at the kitchen table. I just finished making a sandwich and was a few bites in.

As the man walked by, he put his hand on my right shoulder. "Your mother is a wonderful woman." The grin on his face was sick.

I hated him. I didn't care he just brought food for us and I hadn't eaten in three days. There's no charity in the event. My mother accepted this fate out of survival.

The knife I used to cut the sandwich caught my attention. I clutched the knife, slid his hand off my shoulder, placed it on the table, and stabbed the man in the middle of his hand.

I could hear my mother standing near the entrance to the hallway, "Oh my god, Brock!" She looked as though she were about to faint.

A yelp of pain spewed from his mouth. There's no doubt he wasn't expecting a ten-year-old to attack a full-grown man. But there I was, gripping the knife and daring him to make a move.

I anticipated his retaliation. With his free hand, he struck me across the face. I shifted my weight back to decrease the impact. As his hand swept across my face, I pulled the knife away, so I wouldn't lose the valuable weapon. I performed a backward somersault and popped into a defensive stance poised for another assault. I kept my feet balanced just how Vincent always taught me. Instead of retaliating, his response surprised me. He looked amused as though he was anticipating the punch line to a joke. He laughed.

The man ripped the sleeve off his shirt and bandaged his hand. He looked over at my mother and said, "Well, this one has the spunk. I'll tell Quentin about this one. He'll recruit him soon."

The horror on my mother's face was a punch in the stomach. She knew I'd eventually work for Quentin, but when this man spoke the words, it became real. My father died working for Quentin. She feared I'd suffer the same fate. If she lost her husband and her son, what else would she have to live for?

Before leaving our apartment, the man turned around. "If you do that again, you're going to get more than a backhand to the face." He didn't intimidate me. He was a weak man. However, since that day, Quentin kept a special eye on me.

- Chapter 8 -

"Dammit Brock, are you listening to me?" My mother's pained voice breaks through.

Guilt wells up inside me. It's my turn to avert her gaze. She has every right to worry about me. When working for Quentin, anything can happen. There may be a day when I don't return.

I walk over and embrace her. "I'm sorry. I just want you to know you don't need to do that for me. You already do so much."

Choking back her tears she says, "Don't worry about me, just take care of yourself. Promise?"

"Promise," I say making my voice sound as convincing as possible.

I think about my failure to get her medicine yesterday. I'm ashamed. "The price of your medicine increased, and I couldn't afford it yesterday." My voice quickens and rushes to the good news. "But I was able to sell inside the Forum. I'm heading to the dispensary first thing before school."

My mother laughs. "You're so critical of yourself. Thank you." She runs her hand down the side of my face. "Now enjoy your breakfast before it gets cold."

I savor the mouth-watering meal. On my final bite of

bacon, I steal a glance at a picture of my mother and father resting on a shelf. My mother's stomach sticks out. My father has his hand over the top of her stomach with proudest smile. They look genuinely happy even though they live in a prison. My dad died three days after the picture was taken eighteen years ago. The story my mother received of his death aren't clear. She doesn't like to talk about it. Nevertheless, he left his wife and unborn son to survive alone in this hellhole.

I cannot help but despise my father. Why could he not be strong enough to stand here today? I'm here after eighteen years, where is he?

My mother had to find a way to survive after his death. She did what she could. Things got better when I turned thirteen years old. That is the age when young criminals in the Ashen Yard can become a member of a Lord's gang. By becoming a member of Quentin's gang, we no longer pay rent for our apartment. My membership earns us enough to live, but not in luxury.

My mother's voice penetrates my thoughts, "What happened yesterday? You came home late again."

"It took a while to get out of the Forum because someone tried to sneak into the Acropolis." I recount yesterday's events in the Forum. My mother smiles when I talk about returning the lady's wallet. I end the recap at my drawing spot.

"I see," she says. "Was something troubling you?" She knows that drawing is my main coping mechanism.

I think about my drawing. I'm not sure what emotions instructed my hand to draw the image of the young boy.

I deflect her question. "The good news is I sold a couple of drawings yesterday. No jobs, alright? I've got things handled for now."

She nods and I notice the relief.

"I'm serious," I say. "You're always taking care of me. Let me return the favor."

She coughs. "I know. I appreciate it."

I wipe my face clean. A sigh from the satisfying meal escapes my mouth before I tell her I need to go.

"Don't forget your belt," she says.

"Already done," I say as it snaps into place.

My mother gives me a hug and a soft kiss on the check. "Be careful," she says.

My confident smile radiates as I walk out the door.

At the dispensary, I complete the identification process. The lovely female voice comes through the speaker, "How may I assist you today, Brock?"

"I'm here for the prescription."

"I'm glad you were able to get the credits." Her voice sincere. "I was worried for you."

Her comment stuns me. "Really?"

A moment of silence ensues. I'm guessing she needs to be careful not to get too chatty with criminals. "Well, yeah," she begins, "I know this is for your mother."

At that moment I realize how much I enjoy talking to her. She shares the same kindness as my mother.

I scratch my head. "That's kind of you." I insert my payment card and wait for the transaction to process. The air suction noise gurgles as the medicine travels down the tube. A small clunk hits and the metal door opens revealing a small container. I clutch the medicine tight as though it might slip from my grasp. "Thank you."

"Of course," she replies. "I hope you have a great day."

I sign off, run back to my apartment, and drop off the medicine before heading toward the Hub. Walking down the grime filled streets, I look up above and gaze beyond our boundaries. The tops of skyscrapers stick out beyond the barriers of the Ashen Yard. The buildings look magnificent. I often wonder if the people at the tops of these buildings look down upon us. Maybe our miserable lives entertain them.

The Hub appears in the distance. It's like Quentin's castle. The Lords crave control. They use people, like me, to maintain their power. Before I was born, my fate was predetermined. If I didn't become a useful tool to Quentin, I wouldn't be alive. There is no room for the weak in the Ashen Yard.

The Hub is one of the more elegant buildings. By elegant, I mean it's not fully rundown. Any property important to Quentin is well kept. The Hub is where I attend school. This is not a traditional school such as the ones in the Acropolis. The schools where children are taught mathematics, reading, writing, and participate in extracurricular activities. Here I learn survival skills such as how to shoot to kill, use a knife, and engage in hand-to-hand combat. My education revolves around becoming a deadly weapon.

Quentin wants us to kill when we engage in combat. I only do if my life depends on it. I incapacitate my enemy whenever possible. I don't want to take a life. This is my safeguard against becoming the lifeless, soulless criminals who look as dead inside as their gray eyes. I will not be consumed by the system.

Of course, much of the credit goes to my mother for her compassion and love she holds for me. She teaches me how to be a constructive person.

Standing atop the steps of the Hub, I hit the buzzer and make eye contact with the camera. Within seconds I hear a buzz and the lock unlatches. I breathe in and mentally prepare myself. Pulling on the handle, I enter the Hub.

- Chapter 9 -

The entrance to the Hub opens into a grand foyer. An enormous marble water fixture of Quentin sits in the center of him holding a gun in each hand, and water pours out of the barrels. Lined up along both sides of the room are doors evenly spaced apart that lead to the different sections of school. An enormous central staircase leads to the second floor. Only people who are in Quentin's close circle are allowed access to the second floor – a status I have yet to reach.

The Hub is shaped like a giant square with an outdoor courtyard in the center. A lengthy stretch of rooms run along the outer rim. Some of the rooms are regular classrooms for lecture. Others are gyms for exercise and fighting arenas.

The usual ruckus fills the main lobby. Scores of kids huddle in different groups and chatter before lessons. There are times when we meet in a large group, but for the most part, lessons are completed with kids around the same age. In one corner there are the thirteens and fourteens, who are in the infancy of their careers in the gang. In another corner are the fifteens and sixteens staying together in a tightly packed group. Finally, the last group consists of the seventeens and eighteens where I belong.

As it is every morning, I'm in no mood to talk. I don't have friends because friendship seems like a tireless waste of energy. Any friendships I developed over the years always ended in tragedy. My friends' deaths would pull at my heart strings. Eventually, I severed my friendships and kept to myself. Mourning over the inevitable deaths of friends became cumbersome when I have so much more to worry about.

A couple of the eighteens look in my direction. We acknowledge our presence with a nod. To the right is the bulletin board with the daily schedule posted. First on the agenda is lecture, followed by hand-to-hand combat, and finally, target practice. My hands fidget in anticipation for hand-to-hand combat. In a world where there is so much out of my control, it feels good to engage in something where I have control.

While enjoying my solitary status, a younger recruit approaches me out of the corner of my eye. Suddenly, my fingernails look interesting. I hope he gets the hint. I don't have to worry when one of the head instructors, Tank, cracks his knuckles, an infamous sound. The entire hall falls silent. His knuckles mean shut your mouth or get your face smashed. Tank gets his name from his massive size standing at six and a half feet tall. I've seen him twist bones like they are twigs. His dark body is full of tattoos and his biceps are the size of my head. His face always looks like he's going to pop a vein. A scar loops around his right eye. The story behind the scar is Quentin came in just in time to save Tank from getting his eye carved out. With all that said, there is no doubt Tank's presence is intimidating.

His bloodshot eyes scan the room. He screams like a drill sergeant. "Quit yo bellyachin' and report to your stations!" The veins in his neck pulsate. His chest heaves, and he practically foams at the mouth. The morning meeting with Quentin must've been sour.

Everybody knows they need to move, but they're frozen in place by Tank's outrage. They look at him with wide eyes; apart from me, I walk toward my room assignment.

Tank pulls out his gun and points it toward the ceiling. Three rounds fire. "What you waitin' fo? On the double!" His voice shakes the light fixtures.

As if their on-buttons were pushed, everyone scurries toward their rooms. Some recruits run into each other. The sight is comical. A few younger recruits get kicked in their butts as they move past Tank. One of them face plants onto the floor.

When I enter the lecture room, Vincent, my instructor, stands at the front of the room. Vincent is a thin man with a wry smile. He stands just shy of six feet. His mound of red hair falls in a mess around his face. He constantly brushes the hair from his eyes. His nose is long and pointy like a bird's beak, and resting upon his nose are a pair of small glasses. Vincent isn't an impressive human specimen like Tank, but when he fights, he's just as dangerous. His movements are short, quick, and destructive. He's calm even in the most dangerous situations. His emotions hide under a mask. I gave up trying to read him long ago.

Vincent is the one other person in which I care about. Before I became a gang member, he'd appear periodically and teach me. He taught me everything I know about survival. He'd always test my grit and push me beyond my limits. I appreciate his approval. During training sessions, he always pays extra attention to my performance, always providing his sage advice.

Desks line up into compact rows. Lectures contain information about battle strategy or the events happening in the Ashen Yard. Everyone takes a seat and waits for Vincent's voice.

He clears his throat. "As you all know, there is growing tension between Valentine and Quentin."

Quentin and Valentine are the two powerful Lords. There's no love lost between them.

My ears listen to his lecture. "Rumor has it there are smaller rogue groups working together. They use hit and run tactics. Everyone's pointing fingers. There's whisper of war." I doubt Quentin is taking this well.

Vincent pauses and watches the information sink in. He continues, "There's speculation that the smaller groups are recruiting certain prisoners. And why might you ask?"

We look at Vincent with anticipation.

"Every person gone missing is Prisonborn." Once he finishes the statement, his eyes meet mine.

Voices chatter. I hope he's not looking for answers, because I have no idea what's happening. I look around the room and see other Prisonborns. They look as confused as I am.

"We are not sure what to do with this information, yet," says Vincent. "But we're going to continue our daily activities. Our first physical activity today is hand-to-hand combat."

All conversations cease. Everyone tries to put on their best stony look of confidence. No one wants to show weakness. As everyone in the room knows, there's no room for weakness in the Ashen Yard.

"Well, what are you all waiting for?" Vincent barks. "Do I need to fire my gun too? Get suited up and meet me at the Ring in ten."

We disperse out of the room and head toward the locker room. I can't wait to fight.

- Chapter 10 -

Simple gym clothes rest in my locker. I only need the athletic shorts. As I grab them, someone bumps me and knocks me off balance. I don't have to look to know who it is, Tony. He laughs with his buddies.

Tony glowers. "You better watch yourself today. I plan to be the number one around here." He turns and gets confirmation from his buddies.

Tony's targeted me since day one. His desperate want to earn membership to Quentin's inner circle is near embarrassing. No matter how he performs, I always beat him. This doesn't help his burning hatred.

During school sessions, he tries his best to take shots at me. He stays away from me outside of school because he knows how valuable I am to Quentin, and he'd be dead if he messed with me.

I shake my head and start to change. "You sound nervous," my voice calm. "Must be the fear."

I hit a nerve. How satisfying. I slip on the shorts and saunter past keeping a fierce gaze on the band of idiots. Tony fakes a move toward me. I don't flinch. I wink before heading into the Ring.

The Ring is like an old-time boxing gym. A couple of

fighting rings are spread along the massive room, with one featured in the center. There are jump ropes, punching bags, and other exercise equipment laid out for warm-ups. A couple of lap lines circle the outer walls. Some of the recruits are already sparring, jogging, and stretching.

I jog a couple of laps to get my blood flowing before moving to one of the punching bags. My fists pound away until my skin perspires. Static stretching completes my warm-up. I'm ready to fight.

Vincent calls everyone to the center fighting ring. He pairs everyone with a fighting partner. "Brock, you will fight Tony," he says at the end.

I'm satisfied. The heated rivalry between us is no mystery. I'll make him look like a fool, vengeance for the locker room.

Tony and I make eye contact. It's apparent he wants to intimidate me. No matter how hard he tries, it fails. He's done nothing to make me fear him.

We're slated to fight last. In the meantime, we get the simple pleasure of watching others fight. Shouts and taunts fly like the punches in the Ring. Some of the bouts last a couple of minutes, while others are done within a matter of seconds.

My fight is next. Moving to a punching bag, I pound it for a minute to regenerate the blood flow. The final bout finishes as I jog back over. My head turns in a circular motion and I rotate my arms to loosen up. A few shadow punches and my name's called. I climb the ropes.

Tony and I get a mouth guard. This is the only protection we receive during Ring fights. Gloves and head protection are saved for sparring. Nevertheless, cuts, bruises, and the occasional broken bone happen here. Vincent monitors the fights to make sure it doesn't get out of hand. This training is for the field, teaching us how to take a beating.

I steal a glance at Tony. He high fives his buddies before entering the Ring. He smiles red, from the mouthguard, and points in my direction. "You're going down this time," he sneers while hopping up and down.

My head shakes and I laugh. We meet in the center. I stand an inch or two taller than him. Our body builds are nearly identical–athletic and chiseled.

"Alright boys, you know the rules," says Vincent.

We both nod and bump fists.

"Ready. Fight!" yells Vincent. Following the announcement, the spectators shouts surge the Ring.

To commence the fight, Tony charges toward me like an enraged rhino. Poised for his attack, I simply sidestep and smack the back of the head, sending him toward the ground. He springs back to his feet. His eyes on fire.

My moves are calculated. I made him look like a fool in front of everyone, and he knows it was intentional. I'm going to win. I want to let Tony think he stands a chance.

He comes toward me again, this time with more composure. Jabs and hooks come my direction. It's not difficult to dodge Tony's attacks because he lacks discipline. Instead of being patient and graceful, he always engages with brute force. Without discipline, it leaves his body vulnerable.

A quick punch connects on his right side. He leans his body to his right after the blow, and it leaves his face open. Holding back on the power, I release a hook across his face. Red tinted saliva flies out of his mouth.

Tony falls back dazed. Gathering his wits, he looks at me, and this time my smile greets him. Angry eyes respond to my taunts. It's satisfying toying with him. He prepares to come at me again, and this time he means business. I decide I'll let Tony connect with one punch. A little confidence boost before I finish him won't hurt.

He charges and swings furiously. I dodge the blows, wearing him down. I allow one punch to connect with my abdomen. I flex, timing it just as the punch lands. Something is wrong. The force penetrates through my core, knocking the wind out of me. I stagger back and fall to the ground. An invisible force diverts the air away from my lungs.

Just like me, the rest of the class is shocked by the turn of events. Cheers explode from Tony's friends.

Tony pounces on me and pins me at my waist. The striking confidence pulses from his eyes. His left hand grips my neck. He raises his right hand to pummel my face.

That's when I notice it. A shining light flashes from Tony's right hand. What a cheat. That explains how his punch packed serious heat.

His right fist sails toward my face. I muster enough strength and lift my left arm to deflect the punch. The punch misses my face and connects with the ground. He swung with the force to shatter a brick followed by the sickening crunch of broken bones. A yelp and a grimace scrunches his face. His grip loosens and provides a window of opportunity.

I dislodge his hand, grab hold of his shoulders, pull his face toward me, and head butt his nose.

Eyes glazed, he rolls to the ground. Blood pours out of his nose. I'd bet it's broken like his hand. Tony's right fist unclenches, and a steel rod rolls off his fingers.

"Fights over," yells Vincent. He points to Tony. "Get him cleaned up and take him to the med room."

Tony's buddies grab him.

"Everybody clean up and meet me in the courtyard," Vincent barks.

Everyone abides his command. Vincent approaches and puts his hand on my shoulder. "You had me worried. I thought you might actually lose." He moves his hair from his eyes. "You let him punch you, didn't you?"

I huff and cannot help let a grin escape. "Yes. And I learned my lesson."

Vincent breathes in, "I know you're confident Brock, and you trust your abilities, but you really need to be careful, especially the missing Prisonborns." His eyes look above his glasses. "You're not invincible." His tone is like a father talking to his son.

Not sure how to respond, the only word that comes out is, "right." I turn toward the exit.

Everyone's changed back into their regular clothes and funnel toward the courtyard. Vincent's already waiting. Handguns rest on top of tables. The metal of the guns gleam in the sunlight. Most recruits wait in line for a weapon. I skip the line because I already have mine.

Vincent stands behind a table with the ammunition. I reach the counter with an outstretched hand. Vincent pauses and gives me a look. "Quentin has a special lesson for you today." He adjusts his glasses and avoids eye contact.

My eyes narrow. "A special lesson?" My heartbeat thumps.

"Yes," a hint of annoyance laces his voice. His fingers slide under his glasses as he rubs his eyes. "Just wait along the side. I'll escort you to his office shortly."

A few of the recruits hear the conversation and look at me. Their expressions bare envy. That's not how I feel. Uneasiness boils in my stomach. My muscles tense. I want my instincts to be wrong, but they've provided me eighteen years of life. I trust them, and they're telling me to protect myself.

- Chapter 11 -

Vincent finishes distributing the ammo and prompts his assistants to watch target practice. He gestures for me to follow him.

We reach the forbidden stairs in the main lobby. I hesitate as Vincent takes the first few steps. He turns around and says, "What're you waiting for?"

The sunken feeling in my stomach to go away. My first step up feels illegal. I hold the railing for balance.

At the top, we turn right toward a large door. Vincent uses his security card to access the unknown. The top floor doesn't look much different than the bottom. I'm not sure what I was expecting. A long hallway stretches with doors lining both sides.

Our destination is a couple hundred feet. Vincent presses the buzzer and says, "I have Brock." A low buzz and a click. Vincent grabs the handle and opens the door.

A massive form casts an eclipse in the room, Tank. His arms are crossed and his biceps look like basketballs. Beside his towering figure is the Lord himself, Quentin.

Quentin looks ancient with thinning gray hair. His small glasses project an innocent, elderly look. He uses a white wooden cane to walk. The cane is a guise complimenting his façade. A psychotic twitch jerks his head to the side. This happens more frequently the more his anger escalates. He's every bit as dangerous as Tank. He captures the definition of don't judge a book by its cover.

Quentin is a malfunctioning time bomb. Even though the timer ticks, one wrong move can ignite a scary explosion. The first day I attended school, Quentin gave a speech to the new recruits meant to soil ourselves. Trying to appear tough, one of the young boys made a quiet, snide comment to the boy next to him. Without a second thought, Quentin pulled out his handgun and shot the boy in the leg. The other boy received the end of Quentin's cane. Everyone stood still as statues. A couple recruits did soil themselves; others had quivering lips and eyes of fearful tears. I didn't flinch or breakdown. I stood straight and stared forward. I didn't dare allow my tickling fear to surface. I'd gotten good at this by thirteen.

With one boy sobbing, the other whimpering, Quentin glared at everyone, a look that could pierce an angel's soul. His head twitched, "Anyone else have something they'd like to say?" Deadly silence. He laughed. Not like he thought the situation was funny, but like a crazy person. He pointed to Vincent, "Get these pathetic losers cleaned up."

Quentin breaks my memory with his slithering voice, "Welcome." An unwelcoming grin traces his face. I don't respond and his head twitches.

I must respond. I supplement with a nod. I don't respect a man who uses fear to get what he wants. However, I need to be careful because he can make my life miserable.

"I hear you are quite the sharpshooter," he continues, "I personally want to catch a display of your skills."

I'm at a loss for words. Out of the corner of my eye Vincent shifts. A sign of discomfort? I wish he would've told me what is happening.

Quentin lets out a small, twisted laugh. "Not the talker I

see. No matter, please follow us." He uses his cane to point. "Tank, lead the way."

Tank gives a gracious bow of the head and leads us out of Quentin's office. We march down the hallway and make a left turn continuing down a corridor of doors.

My eyes analyze Quentin's gait. He uses his cane with each step with no visible limp.

"Oh, this will be wonderful," Quentin cackles to the air. "I've been so bored lately. This will mark my day." After his small monologue, he looks over his shoulder with a wink.

I shiver. My gut was right. Vincent stands next to me. I attempt to make eye contact a few times, but he stares forward.

Our destination looms before us. Tank uses his card to open the door.

The room is a conference room about five hundred square feet with a long oval table in the center and chairs lining the table. This must be a tactical room. Why there are so many chairs is beyond me. Quentin's inner circle consists of Tank, Vincent, and a few others who stay behind the scenes. Maybe Quentin has more firepower than we know.

My eyes circle the room. A couple of guards take position along the walls. My eyes make it to the other end of the room, and I freeze, someone strapped to a chair. He's bound and gagged with blood trailing down the side of his face. The blue shirt indicates he's one of Valentine's. He looks about the same age as me. Recognition pounds my memory. He's the one who attempted to be friendly after the incident in the Forum, and I dismissed him. Why the hell is he here?

- Chapter 12 -

Quentin's eyes cheer with delight while the eyes of the young man strapped to the chair scream fear. My stomach knots and I almost kneel over in pain.

"You're quite impressive," Quentin says to me. "I've been keeping an eye on your progress. Your marks are the highest of anyone who's had the pleasure of representing me." He looks at me like I should be proud of my accomplishments.

I stay silent.

He continues, "You're practically the perfect weapon. But are you loyal?" He lingers on the question and places his hand on his chin. "Is your gun loaded?"

I stare at the young man lost in a dream. Beads of sweat form on my brow. Vincent nudges me from behind. Quentin's eye twitches. I nod.

"Most excellent," Quentin says with a pleased smile. "Now listen and listen carefully." His voice gets deadly quiet like he's passing on valuable information meant only for my ears. "I'm going to give you a set of directions, and you will follow them. Understood?"

Another nod.

"If you're to be in my inner circle, you'll learn to respond to your master," Quentin booms with a twitch.

He swings his cane. I see it coming and could easily dodge

it but take the hit. It feels like the right choice. The splintered wood whips across the back of my thigh. A searing pain shoots up my body. I bite my lip.

"Yes, sir," I force through clenched teeth.

"Yes, master," he mocks.

"Yes, master," I return with a hint of sarcasm. The comment does not seem to faze Quentin.

A wicked smile and a laugh, "Very good. This is going to be most excellent." His fingers fiddle together. "Alright, first order." The air thickens. It's difficult to breathe. "Take aim and shoot this treacherous man in his left shoulder between the tendons that connect the arm to the body."

My face stays still but my insides scream. He expects a good soldier to follow orders without second thought. I don't want to be a good soldier. I work for him out of convenience. The money helps take care of my mother. This man is a psycho. He's the image Pawns draw when they imagine a criminal from the Ashen Yard. It's the men like him who helped create this place.

I look at the young man. His eyes are wide. Tears run down his cheeks. My sorrow so thick it could be thrown. This is unnecessary. There's no sense of honor in this. Any violence in my life is based on the need to survive. It hits me. In a sick, twisted way, hurting this young man is necessary for my survival. If I don't follow through, the consequences will fall upon me. I struggle with the pity for the victim and the disgust for what I must do. My swirl of emotions stay hidden with a stony expression, not a single tremor in my body.

I take a chance. "There's no honor in this." Quentin's head jerks and Tank and Vincent nearly jump. "Why are you insulting me?" This time Vincent puts his hand on my shoulder. I remove it and continue my thought, "Why are you testing my accuracy on someone who is bound like a simple target? If you want to see my skills, test me in battle."

Quentin's look shouts treason. It shifts to amusement. He

laughs maniacally. "Is that defiance I smell?" He pulls out his gun and points it at me. "Tread carefully." His gun clicks. "You'll have plenty of time to display your skills in battle."

With a breathless apology I raise my gun, take aim, and fire, square in the shoulder. A muffled scream pulsates through the gag. He tries to jerk loose from his bindings but to no avail. Blood runs down his arm. Within seconds, the screams turn into small whimpers.

"Check the shot," Quentin barks at the guards.

One of the guards looks at the shot and says, "Exactly where you instructed, master."

My fate with Quentin is sealed.

He's pleased and cackles gleefully. "The stories about you are true." Sick, twisted pleasure washes his face. "What a delicious treat. Now for the second order. Shoot him in the right leg just below his kneecap." His look of anticipation is disgusting.

A tiny gulp settles my throat. Again, I raise my gun and hide the emotions pummeling my insides. No tension, no nervousness, just action.

The second round fires. I'm a good little sheep. More screams burst out of the man's mouth. He tries to plead through his gag.

I hate Quentin.

"Oh, this is perfect," Quentin squeals. "This is most exciting." He bounces like a giddy child.

Quentin's eyes gaze up toward the ceiling. I can see the dark twisted cloud hovering inside his head. All the while, the man continues a muffled plea for his life.

Although it is only seconds, it feels like an eternity before Quentin speaks again. "Now kill him." He says it nonchalantly disregarding the value of a life.

The words bounce around in my head. Even though this is the logical outcome of the situation, it still catches me by surprise. He wants me to complete the test with excellent marks.

I scream at Quentin inside my head. My mind plays a scenario where I aim the gun at him and fire. The scenario ends with my death. Perverse pleasure washes over his face. His right eye twitches.

"I have one request." My voice commanding. He doesn't own me.

The pleasure drains from his face. Another twitch, veins pop, a line is crossed.

"What is it?" his question hisses through his teeth.

"I want this man's name."

The request makes Quentin falter. The fury wipes clean off his face. This may sound odd, but it's important to me.

Another maniacal laugh erupts, increasing the tension in the room by a few degrees. Tank stands perplexed, Vincent uncomfortable. My small act of defiance sets an interesting stage. "This is great," Quentin says. "What a treasure. What the hell. Go ahead, ask his name."

I simply call out, "Agent of Valentine, what's your name?" The guards realize he cannot answer with a gag, and they remove it. Sobs and whimpers flow from his mouth. He doesn't respond to my request. Knowing his name is important. I repeat the request again increasing the volume of my voice. Again, no response, something I cannot blame him for.

Quentin fidgets. My time's nearly up. Looking at the guards, I make one final desperate attempt. "Please check his tag." Quentin nods and the guard moves. "Jared," he says.

"Last name?"

A sigh of annoyance and one last check. "Sutton."

"Alright, you have his name." Quentin pulls his gun. "Now execute your task." His eyes slice through my body.

I poise my gun to shoot. Without the slightest tremor, I raise my gun and take careful aim at the man's chest. No more suffering. It's time to finish this. Before I shoot, my eyes burn toward Quentin. Exhaling slowly, the pull of the trigger ignites a burst. My eyes fixed on Quentin. A direct hit, no more whimpers, and the deed is done. My eyes take a steely glance toward the man then back to Quentin.

He bounces in his chair like he just received the perfect gift. “I love it.” A smile that says *I'm pleased with your actions* extends my way. A switch turns and his expression changes to boredom. “You're dismissed.”

The door signals my exit. Vincent stays on my heels. My shoulder jerks back before I can get too far. “Remember what I said about being confident. Why are you trying to be Mr. Bravado with Quentin? You're playing with fire.”

“I know what I'm doing.” My voice comes out coarse and shaky faltering any glimpse of confidence.

“I don't think you realize what you're dealing with.” His eyes rage with a spark about to burst.

I brush his comments to the side, break free, and run. My eyes tunnel for the exit of the Hub. My mind tries to comfort my thoughts, telling me the faster I separate myself from this event, the easier it will be to forget. My momentum pushes me through a forceful exit. My legs gain speed on my way home with the burning image of Jared bleeding from his chest.

- Chapter 13 -

My legs burst into a sprint the closer I am to home. No matter how many times I must kill, it doesn't get easier. Each time feels like the first. This feeling is how I know I'm still human.

My apartment comes into vision. The despair and rage consume my being. All that swallows my mind is Quentin's smug face. Somehow, he knew taking the life of the young man would tear me apart. He won – the defeat strips me of my conscience. The reality pummels me. Am I laughing? It harnesses no humor. It isn't crazy, yet. Onlookers roaming the rugged streets stand with leery glances. They avoid eye contact and scatter away like I carry a plague.

Looking up, my hands reach toward the sky. "Why?" I shout. "How? I don't know?" My shoulders shrug, and it must look like I'm having a conversation. "God, this is stupid." My laugh ceases abruptly. My emotions grow cold. My face a rock. I move back into a sprint toward my apartment stairs. Now I'm trying to outrun myself.

I bound up the steps three at a time. I reach the top and stop to gather my wits. Running my hands through my hair, it feels like an eruption like an angry volcano will burst from my chest. My legs bounce up and down releasing adrenaline. A short, forceful yell escapes my mouth before entering the apartment.

When I'm inside, I don't anticipate engaging in any conversation with my mother, except to tell her I'm heading to the Forum to sell my drawings. I sneak my way toward my room to grab my bag when I hear my mother in the bathroom. She's coughing, an unpleasant cough that sounds like it's shaking her entire body.

Guilt wracks me. I'm about to sneak in and out without considering my mother or her health. I clear my throat. "Mom, are you alright?" Instead of a response, more coughing escapes from the bathroom. I almost burst through the door. My mother hunches over the sink, looking haggard and exhausted. She clears her throat and spits red into the sink. Blood.

"What's going on?" I ask in a rushed voice that comes out accusatory. I flush again with guilt. "I'm sorry," I say in a gentler voice and rub her back. "I don't mean to sound like a jerk. You're scaring me."

Two wet trails fall down the sides of her cheeks. She gathers her composure. Her head turns. She forms a weak smile. "Don't be alarmed." Her reassurance fails. "I don't think the new medicine has fully spread through my system. I'm just having a bad day."

"No big deal? Are you serious? You're coughing up blood!"

She dismisses my concerns. "Brock, this isn't the first time I've coughed up blood. This is just the first time you've seen it happen."

I roll my eyes. "As if that's supposed to make me feel better."

She coughs again and spits into the sink. The color of her saliva is a light pink. She hunches over the sink for a few more moments and gathers her breath. She stands up, and I help steady her balance.

"Come on," I say. "Let me walk you to your room so you

can rest." Her energy is depleted. I practically carry her. "Hopefully the medicine kicks in soon." An exasperated laugh escapes from my mouth. What's with the laughing? It's like I want to reassure myself. Reassure myself that my life isn't falling apart.

With careful steps, we make it to her room. I lay her down soft as a cloud and tuck her into bed. She pulls the bed comforter up to her face and shivers.

"I think we have one packet of tea left," I say as I run to the kitchen.

There is indeed one packet of honey tea in the cupboard. I make a note to grab more in the Forum and prepare hot water.

I return to my mother's side, "Once the teas is ready, it will help sooth your throat."

"Thank you," she starts, "I'm going to have a medical reevaluation later this afternoon." Her eyes avert mine.

My face scrunches. "I just got your medicine. Do you need something else?"

She shrugs. "I don't think it's a bad thing to get checked again."

She's hiding something. I know it. My hand rests upon her forehead. Her skin feels clammy. At least she isn't running a fever. "Well, I planned on going to the Forum today, but I can wait and take you to your reevaluation."

"Don't stress about it. I've got it covered." I raise my eyebrows. She musters up enough strength to hit me in the arm. "I have some friends."

Before I can respond, the kettle whistles in the kitchen. "I'll be right back."

I return with a cup of hot tea and help her sit up in bed. She blows on the tea and takes a small sip.

"I should be the one to take you," I say to continue our conversation.

"I just realized the time, why are you home early?" she

says, changing the subject.

The memory of what happened today flashes before my eyes. My respite gone. Jared slumped in the chair, bleeding from three bullet wounds, Quentin maniacally laughing and gaining pure pleasure from his control over me. I think back to Vincent and his odd comment. Well, he doesn't know what *I'm* dealing with. Here I sit with my frail mother trying to keep her as healthy as possible.

My mother expects an answer while I daydream. I muster a weak lie, "Lessons were cut short today, sort of like a half-day."

She looks for a lie and nods. "I appreciate everything you've done for me today, but you don't need to hover over your old mother. I'm feeling better. I know you want to go to the Forum."

I assess her condition. She seems more relaxed and the strength is back in her voice.

She nudges me off the bed. "Quit thinking about it and just go." Her smile looks healthier. Maybe the medicine saturated her system.

I kiss her forehead and leave the apartment with my bag of drawings.

- Chapter 14 -

Once inside the Forum, I set up my vendor booth in the usual spot. The place doesn't bustle with its normal buzz. The incident yesterday impacted the Pawns.

My mind reverts back to Jared. I need to draw him to help me gain closure. Too many lives have died by my hands. I do not number the victims because quantifying the mass only adds to the burden I already carry. I'm fortunate to get Jared's name. In the heat of battle, I'm unable to get the identities of the fallen. I use my visual skills to recreate a moment of time. It's how I ask for forgiveness.

My eyes focus on the canvas. Drawing the events inside the conference room at school is out of the question. Instead, I draw our only other interaction, yesterday's moment. My hands sketch the contours.

The drawing is simple, yet elegant. Jared stands featured in the center walking. His skinny stature draws attention to his prominent face. His jacket is held by his left hand and tossed over his left shoulder. Dark rings tuck under his eyes. His hair slightly ruffled with a few strands falling over his face. His smile is gentle. In the background, the entrance to the Forum blends in with the walls of the prison. Smaller human figures walk in their respective directions. I gleam back, satisfied I gave Jared the justice he deserves.

"Is he a friend?" a strange voice asks in front of me.

My laser focus releases. I look up at the voice and realize there are approximately twenty people gathering around my booth. My gaze casts beyond the huddled crowd and realize how many more people are in the Forum, which seems strange when it appeared to be a ghost town fifteen minutes prior.

"It's no one," I reply.

"I'd like to buy it," says the customer.

I jot Jared's name on the back and put it in my bag. "I'm sorry. It's not for sale."

Murmurs come from the crowd. They talk about my drawings. Customer after customer approaches my booth, and before I know it, I'm immersed in my greatest selling day ever. Credit after credit transfers to my payment card.

The sizable crowd continues to hover around my booth past my final transaction. I look at my payment card. I earned four-hundred and fifty credits. I don't have words.

Impressed with my business, I scan the crowd. My eyes stop on a dime. My heart skips. A stunning girl stands about fifty feet away. She's shopping around the different craft vendors. Her skin is a soft silky white that reflects the light as if she were an angel. Her light brown hair falls past her shoulders in perfect alignment. She wears a simple white shirt with a small pullover yellow sweater. Her skirt, the color of the sky, is modest, passing her knees. Dangling earrings match the color of her skirt flash in the light. Tall white socks reach their way down to her petite yellow shoes. Two silver bangles dance along her wrists. Every gesture she makes seems like an act of grace. Pure stunning grace.

My mind flusters and my heart races. What I'm feeling is unfamiliar. The surge of emotion almost hurts. She turns her head and makes eye contact with me for the briefest moment. Her eyes are of another world. They are a glistening green like a perfect jade, flawless in every fashion possible. Eyes that could end a war. Eyes that make me forget pain.

I'm staring, probably gawking. My cheeks flush. She smiles, and when she does, I wish I could wake up to that face every morning.

There is a shout of a name I can't quite hear over the noise of the customers. She turns and looks behind her. I follow her eyes and see someone waving at her in the crowd. The faded outline of the person hides within the shadows. A small hint of recognition surfaces. Probably a regular roamer of the Forum.

The girl waves before disappearing in the crowd. I stand dumbfounded.

I pace around my booth like I don't know what to do. I'm stunned. My mind isn't functioning properly. Packing up my things, I head back to the Ashen Yard.

Plenty of girls roam around the Forum and Ashen Yard. Never once did I take notice. It's a waste of time. I feel the same way about love as I do friendships. Relationships ultimately end in hardship. Besides, I have no plans to marry and have a family. I will never condemn a child to my world. No offense mother.

There's something different about the girl with the green eyes. It feels like a different person wants to carve itself out of my body. What if this is different? What if I decide to try and make something happen? What if I could experience a relationship, love?

I shake the impossible thoughts out of my head. How stupid. There's no way in this world I could ever be with this girl. She is a Pawn. She's from a forbidden place. What person would abandon the sanctuary of the Acropolis for misery?

Why am I still thinking about her? I brush my thoughts asides. It's time raise the barrier – become emotionless, use my on and off switch.

The entrance to the Ashen Yard looms over me when I

recognize my stone-wall emotional defense isn't staying fortified. A couple of cracks allow her to slip through. I don't know. Maybe.

- Chapter 15 -

I return to my apartment in the early evening. The sun shines a soft, gentle glow that whispers peace. A breeze lightly brushes the surface of my skin. The grass and trees look healthier. My apartment doesn't look as run down. Nature can strip away an ugly façade and show beauty where beauty hides its face. Maybe my vision is blinded by an unusual optimism. There's an uncharacteristic spring in my step. The feelings inside my stomach tear at its walls.

Entering my apartment, my mother sits at the kitchen table. Her mouth moves but my ears don't pick up the sound.

I rush into my room. Throwing my bag onto the bed, I scurry over and position myself in front of the mirror. At least I didn't look totally unkempt. My hair is only slightly messy and my face is clean. I look closely at my eyes. My fingers trace along their features. I hear my mother complimenting them, but I still fail to see her perspective. Soft gray, dark gray, light gray, all just gray. There's no getting around it. They look sad.

After the physical examination, I go back to the kitchen. My mother sits at the dining table. I join her. She doesn't look awful like she did earlier today, but she still looks weaker than normal.

"What's going on?" she asks with raised eyebrows. Shock

lines her face. "Why are you smiling?"

Her question surprises me. Am I smiling? I try to cover it up. "I guess," my words falter, and I realize the extent of my embarrassment. I never have conversations with my mother about girls. When I was younger, she would try to rouse a reaction out of me with prodding questions about girls, but she quit when I didn't respond. She came to terms with my philosophy on relationships.

She looks for an explanation. She wears a smile. She wants to share in the joy.

My thoughts stutter. How do I talk about something I cannot wrap my head around? It hits me. "I made four-hundred and fifty credits today selling my drawings." The comment is greeted with a low whistle. "That's really going to help get your medicine. Speaking of, how was your reevaluation?"

I catch a tiny flinch in my mother's smile, but she holds steady. "I'm not getting better. They prescribed me something different."

"Again?" The anxiety swirls in my stomach. "I just picked up yesterday. Are we getting refunded? We better get refunded, if not." My vision flashes back to my fist fight with the dispensary.

My mother slides her hand across the table and touches mine. It pains me to see how quickly her joy faded.

We both try to stay strong, but sometimes there are only so many blows you can take. "Dammit!" My leg bounces under the table. I pause and hold my hands up to the front of my face like I am praying. "How much is the new medicine?"

"There wasn't a quote."

Anxiety tightens my chest. "No matter, I made more today than I usually do in a month's worth of selling. I'll get it first thing tomorrow." I pause a moment, still in shock. "What's wrong? What is the diagnosis?"

"That," she looks toward the counter and pauses as though

she's figuring out how to deliver bad news. "They aren't sure." This is how she ends her explanation. No elaboration.

"How can they figure out how to make you better if they don't even know what's wrong?" I fume. I'm angry. Angry about my mother suffering. Angry about the idiot doctors who can't figure this out. Angry about how no one gives two craps about someone like my mother.

"The doctors need more time. They don't always have the answer, but they're working on a solution. Let's not let this spoil the time we have for dinner."

Being caught in the moment, I didn't even acknowledge the fact my mother prepared food. The aroma settles my thoughts. "Of course."

My mother serves us. Tonight, she whipped up a simple dinner of pasta with a red sauce and garlic bread. I devour the food on my plate.

As I eat, my mind returns to the girl. No matter what I try, I cannot shake her from my thoughts. Love at first sight is such a silly notion. To truly love someone, you need to know them as a whole person.

I don't notice my mother's stare. "You're smiling again. What's really on your mind?"

Talking about a girl stirs my comfort. I deflect. "How did you know father was the one?" I lean back. "Was it based on circumstance, or did you know right away?"

She gets a funny look. We normally don't talk about my father. My mother was crushed when he passed. Despite the pain of losing him, she always seems happy when thinking of him.

She sits there pondering my questions. Her face lights up as she says, "Oh Brock, I knew I loved your father at first sight." Her words feel young. "I remember the first moment I saw him. He was working. He had a large wood beam resting across his neck with both arms wrapped over the top. He wore a cut off white shirt. His muscles bulged. He wore blue jeans and light brown boots that were covered in dirt. As I watched him carry the beam, we made eye contact. He gave me the most gorgeous, trusting smile. His smile held my eyes captive." As she's telling me the story, her eyes lift to the ceiling, and she becomes lost in the memory.

My mind tries to get a clearer image of the event. "Was father working in the industrial district of the Forum?"

My mother snaps out of her daze. She falters a second before responding. "The industrial district," she says almost as though she were asking a question. "Oh yes, of course. From that moment, I knew I loved your father."

"How did you know? You know, without actually knowing him?"

She laughs. "I don't know if I can answer that question. It's one of those things you feel. There was this kindness and comfort. It was like he could pull me in with his own gravitational pull." The joyous smile returns. "I don't know if I answered your question, but that's how I felt."

I scratch my head. "I guess so." Her eyes lose focus again, another memory. "He was a lucky man."

Her eyes flicker. "And I an equally lucky lady." Curiosity spreads. "What's really on your mind?"

The heat rushes to my cheeks. She sniffs out my embarrassment.

"Who's the lucky lady?"

"Well. I. There is." Come on words. Why won't you form? I gather my composure. "I saw this girl in the Forum. There was just something about her that was captivating." I tell her the intricate details.

After I finish telling my mother, she sighs, "Did you talk to her?"

I shake my head. "I kind of wanted to, but there is one major problem."

"Which is?"

"Her eyes are green." She knows what that means.

Her look changes to sympathy. She's about to speak, but I don't give her the chance. "I don't need you to feel sorry for me. Besides, I don't even know the girl. I glanced at her for a few seconds. Really, what more is it than infatuation?" My stomach churns. My words try to convince me, but my heartache tells another story.

We are interrupted by an air horn. My eyes light up. This alarm requires me to gear up and go to the Hub. There's no doubt I will engage in combat.

I speed into my room to gather my necessities. With my gun belt strapped around my waist, I march toward the apartment door.

"This isn't fair," my mother says. "Our moment interrupted."

I laugh. "Since when is anything fair around here?"

She coughs a few times. "Take this along the way." She tears off a sizable chunk of bread and hands it to me. She kisses my cheek, and hugs me. "Be careful. Come back so we can finish this conversation."

"Of course," I reply.

- Chapter 16 -

As I approach the Hub, Quentin's gang huddles around awaiting directions. There's a rustle of chatter with a hint of excitement.

Tank stands on the top landing of the Hub with his arms crossed. His massive form stands still like a ghostly silhouette. Vincent emerges from the large entrance and approaches Tank. He speaks in his ear.

After a few moments, Tank nods and barks orders. Everyone files in. The older members of the gang are grouped into squads based on the skills of each member.

Vincent and Tank develop the squads, well, mostly Vincent. He has an untouchable combat intuition. He's like a general. Tank isn't more than a yelling machine who smashes his enemies.

Vincent understands me. He rarely places me in a squad. I work better alone. I rely on myself.

The younger members get sorted by Vincent. Some join existing squads, while others get placed on guard duty. The younger ones try to hide their fear. It's written across their faces.

"Shaddup and listen," Tanks yells and flexes his arms. "There's twos strikes, one norwest, the other souwest. Git ready to smash."

Vincent adjusts his glasses and hair and steps forward. "Let me clarify. The attacks are small. We don't believe they came from Valentine. We'll be active around our perimeter and send scout teams. We must be cautious. We'll give you assignments shortly, but first, everyone gear up."

I grab a few extra magazines. Quickly and efficiently, the gear gets dispersed. Tank keeps barking orders. He likes to hear his voice.

I stand near the veteran members. Tank takes massive steps in our direction. I think he's going to address me, but he towers in front of Tony. I didn't even notice the little weasel.

"Tony, you lead da veterans," Tank says as he tosses Tony a headset. "Git out on patrol."

Tony puffs his chest out. He salutes Tank before jeering at me. "It's my honor, sir!"

"Oh hell," Tank replies. "Dun screw up."

Tony turns around. "Alright boys, you heard him. Have your gear ready and settle fifty yards out. On the double!" This power will walk into his head and make him a bigger pain in the ass.

Tank turns to me. "Quentin likes you. Special task." A crooked grin highlights his face.

Tony hears this and looks back. His temporary moment of smug victory is gone just as it fell upon his fingertips. He looks like a deflated balloon. What he doesn't understand, and I will never let him, is hearing Quentin and special task in the same sentence wrenches my gut.

Tank throws a headset at me. "Number fo. Dun speak unless you needs to."

This is a commander headset. I wrap it around my head and tune to channel four. Channel one is for general chat. Squad leaders use channel two to communicate with their squad. Channel three is for private conversations amongst squad leaders.

Now I have access to the legendary channel four. It makes

me question my responsibilities. My last loyalty check crosses my mind, the image of Jared bleeding and bound to a chair. His haunting eyes plead for mercy.

Tanks slaps me on the back and the wind is knocked out of me. "Aight loner."

Vincent joins us and intervenes, "I've got it from here."

Tank looks offended at first, and I expect him to go on an angry rant. Instead, he pouts, which looks funny for a man his size.

"Whatevs," Tank mutters and walks away.

I never really thought about Vincent and Tank's relationship. These two have worked closely together for as long as I can remember. There's a tension I can feel.

Vincent puts his hand on the back of my neck and gives it a squeeze. "Alright, listen carefully." His face is stern. "Quentin wants you to scout in the southwest sector. He trusts you can investigate to provide us with intelligence." He pauses a moment to make sure I'm paying attention. My eyes lock on his. "We think something big is happening. It's imperative you keep open communication." He turns so his back faces Tank. Grabbing my hand, he forces my palm open. He places something cool and hard in it and closes my fingers.

"What," is all I get out before Vincent silences me with his hand.

"It belongs to you," he says. "You ready?"

I stick whatever Vincent handed me into my pocket. "Yes, sir."

"Remember, communicate," Vincent reinforces.

Tank walks over. "Shoots to kill." A failed attempt to become a part of the conversation.

I head toward my destination.

- Chapter 17 -

While I run, I reach into my pocket searching for the object Vincent handed me. My fingers fumble across it. Pulling it out of my pocket, I stop in my tracks. It's a necklace. I grab my flashlight to get a better look. Hanging from the end of the chain is a gold shield. On the shield are swords, one standing vertical and two crossing over it diagonally.

What's the story behind this? Why does it belong to me? I flip it over. It looks like there used to be an inscription, but it's worn. The only visible word is *hood.*

Gunshots snap me out of my reverie. I shut off my flashlight and ready my handguns. The shots came from a distance, so the threat isn't immediate. I look in the direction of the shots. Thick vegetation lies across the flat land. I mentally mark my destination.

A crackle hisses in my ear. "I haven't heard from you," the voice is Vincent. "Give me a status update."

I press the mic button. "Shots fired. Going to investigate. Not much else to report."

"Be careful," Vincent replies with a bit of strain. "Just communicate."

I take advantage of this opportunity. "What's the story with this necklace? If it belongs to me, why did you have it?"

There's a long silence. I begin to think he didn't hear me. He breaks the silence. "It's special, and now is not the time. Focus on the task at hand."

I hide the disappointment, "Roger." My focus returns on what's in front of me. More shots fire. My speed increases.

An area of thicker trees approaches. Flashes of light correspond with gunshots. I crouch down to analyze the situation. A silhouette of a human figure backs up against a tree with a gun in hand. They peek around the tree and fire and retreat back behind the tree. Looking in the direction of the shots, another silhouette outlines in the darkness. The outline looks unusual. It looks like a soldier. The darkness is playing tricks on me.

The outfit of the person hidden behind the tree is a simple shirt and pants. The shirt is a lighter color than mine. It must be a member of Valentine's gang.

I slither toward the person behind the tree. My footsteps are productive, yet silent. Dealing with two potential enemies means I must be precise.

My approach easy. I get within twenty feet when Valentine's member peeks around the tree and fires. Here's my chance, but I freeze. My target takes two shots to his chest and falls to the ground completely still.

I hear feet shuffle. I flatten on the ground. Within seconds, two figures emerge from the trees and stoop over the body. Even in the dimness of the night, I can tell they are different. They do look like soldiers in uniforms. A grayish camouflage pattern stretches along the uniform. A heavy looking backpack lays strapped across their backs. Round, hard helmets rest upon their head. They hunch over the body. I feel the urge to make a move, but one of them speaks.

"Is this one of them?" one of the soldiers asks.

The other one takes out a device. The screen illuminates in the darkness. He fiddles with the screen and a red light shines from the back. They're doing something with the eyes.

The red light scans across the face.

"Well?" asks the one without the handheld.

"Negative," his companion replies.

A small moan escapes from the body and it moves. The one who seems in charge pulls out a gun and shoots. The body almost bounces off the ground and lies still for the second time.

More gunshots burst through the trees. This draws the attention of the two suspicious characters. They leave the area.

Once they stretch out of sight, I crawl to the body. When I get there, I observe he is young, no older than fifteen. What baffles me is I only see one bullet wound. I know it's dark, but I swear he was shot at least three times. Why is there only one wound?

My curiosity peaks, and I lift his shirt. Along with the bullet wound, two large welts rise off the surface of the skin and almost look like large blisters. The welts are bruised from shots that didn't penetrate the skin. I try to put two and two together when more shots fire. I curse myself for lowering my guard in a hot zone.

A crackle buzzes in my ear reminding me I'm connected to Vincent. I open communication. "There are strangely dressed people fighting Valentine's agents. They look like soldiers."

"I see," replies Vincent. There's a brief pause. The static crackles in my ear and I only catch the tail end of what he says, "...ening."

"I didn't copy."

"Dammit," Vincent says. "Report back to the Hub."

My mind floods with questions. They wanted me to investigate. I find something and they call me back? I decide to keep investigating.

The gunshots are quiet. Crawling up to the same tree the young boy used, I rise to my feet with my handguns ready. I peer around the tree to spot any movement. For the moment, everything is silent and still. Clusters of trees litter the area with tall grass gently swaying in the night's breeze. I concentrate my energy on my hearing. Nothing. The night appears at peace.

Crouching again, I take small steps in the direction of the last shots. Movement disturbs some trees about forty feet away stopping me frozen in my tracks. Two of the gray dressed soldiers emerge from the trees. They're dragging someone. They both hold onto the person's wrists. It looks like another one of Valentine's. A faint moan comes from the man.

I lie down in the protection of the tall grass and thank the dark. I aim one of my handguns and shoot at a tree near them. I got their attention.

"Get down!" one of them yells. They flatten themselves like me. Their packs stick above the grass.

They appear disoriented. I crawl in their direction. I'm curious as to why they dragged one body but killed the other. I halt my advance. Ten others make a formation along the trees holding their weapons.

I don't care for these odds. I kick myself for not listening to Vincent. This could be the end.

Just backtrack to the protection of a tree and make a run for it. With each backward crawl, I watch the mysterious persons. Then bright lights illuminate the surroundings. One light shines in my face. Time to get the hell out of here.

"There!" one of them yells. "Eleven o'clock."

Shots fire. I manage to make it behind the tree. I could run, but they will not be far behind. I'll take a few of them down and show them I'm not someone to mess with.

More bullets pepper the tree. Their flashlights scan across the grass. Their lights are the clues I need. Whipping around the tree, I fire one shot and connect. A piercing yell comes from my target, and he drops his gun. The shot hit him in the shoulder, enough to incapacitate him. I fire a second shot and hit another, this time in the leg before sliding back behind the tree. More shots fire in my direction.

Again, gauging from the lights, I pop around and shoot with deadly aim. Each shot connects with a target, and two of the lights go down. Yowls of pain paint the night.

One of them shouts, “There must be more than one.”

I reinforce their reverie of my skills. Appearing again, I fire and hit another, and as always, nothing lethal.

“Retreat!” I hear. “This isn’t worth it!”

“Cover us,” I hear others say.

The bullets stop. Their movement through the tall grass fades in the distance. I fight every urge to look around the tree. I wait two minutes before running back toward the Hub.

Vincent, and only Vincent greets me. He adjusts his hair and glasses. At first, he’s upset I violated direct orders. Despite his initial anger, he listens to my story. His face looks complacent, not even a flinch. When I finish, he pushes his glasses up.

“You’ve done well,” he says and pats me on the back. “I’ll deliver the report to Quentin. He’ll be pleased.”

“I don’t care if he’s pleased or not. I want some insight.”

“Careful,” Vincent warns. “Go home and get some rest. You deserve it. Come in tomorrow when you get up. There is no official reporting time because of tonight’s events.”

“What’s going on?” I ask. “What I saw isn’t normal.”

“I wish I knew.” Vincent squeezes my shoulder and turns back toward the Hub.

Back at my apartment, I lie on my bed, exhausted. My eyes become fixed on the ceiling. My mind wanders. The unanswered questions float in my head. It doesn’t take long before my world fades. Before I’m asleep, I remember the girl and her gorgeous green eyes. I fall asleep with a smile.

- Chapter 18 -

When I wake up the next morning, everything is quiet, no sounds of my mother's morning routine. I peek inside her room and find an empty bed. Her absence is odd. I wander into the kitchen and find a note on the table.

Brock,

I was relieved to see you home safe this morning. I have a few errands to run. I feel better today. I hope we get to continue our conversation. I want to know more about this girl.

Even though you are under the same curse as all of us here, your eyes are different. No matter how hard of a shell you put up, the kindness resides within you. I know this is keeping you from talking to the girl. Why hold back? Chances are a mystery to solve.

Love,

Mom

I'm embarrassed after finishing the note, which seems silly. When I think about the dangers in my life, talking to a girl should be a breeze, but somehow, the mysterious girl flusters me.

I eat a small meal and get ready. With my mind preoccupied on last night's event, I nearly forget about my mother's new medicine. I'll stop by the dispensary before reporting to the Hub. Hopefully my questions about last night will get answered.

Outside, my lungs breathe in the morning. The early sun casts strings of glowing light that bounce off the ground. A thin layer of dew rests upon all surfaces. It smells like a new beginning, providing a gentle reminder of life's beauty. Savoring one more deep, fresh breath, my feet point in the direction of the dispensary.

On my steady walk, the cheery chirps of birds vibrate from the trees. A bird lands on a tree. A worm dangles from its beak. Three baby birds chirp in anticipation for the upcoming meal. Moments like this are meant to be captured. This will make a good drawing.

At the dispensary, I follow the initialization process. My card reminds me of the lucrative sales from, what, yesterday? It seems like a lifetime ago. At any rate, it feels good to have such a large sum of disposable credits. I plan to purchase a few nice things in the Forum for my mother, maybe a comfortable pair of shoes.

"Good morning, Brock," says the lovely voice. So peaceful.

I feel more chipper than usual. My voice bounces. "Good morning." My fingers move to punch in the prescription number, but then realize, I don't have one. "I apologize. I don't know the prescription number."

"No problem. I'll be happy to assist you. Please answer the questions that pop up."

My eyes watch as a question materializes. What is the patient's full name? I type in Laura Mae Anderson. The next question asks for the patient's prisoner identification number. Once I finish, she speaks. "Thank you. Give me a second to pull up the information. How's your day?"

"Nothing out of the ordinary, I guess." Even though her voice is comforting and isn't filled with judgment, it's still awkward to chat. She's different from most Pawns.

"Okay, I found..." her voice squeaks and stumbles. "Do you plan to pay for this today?"

"Of course, why else would I be here?" My stomach turns.

The receiving end is silent for a couple of moments. Another click and sorrow laces her voice, "The prescription will be five thousand credits."

Stunned. Confused. Angry. "Holy...," It feels like someone punched me in the soft part of the stomach. The air siphons out of my lungs. My words fizzle. It takes a few moments to gather my composure. The anger swells within the pit of my stomach. Pounds of pressure presses against my skull. "Are you serious?"

"I'm–"

I don't let her continue. "What the hell is this? What," I linger on the word. "Is the medicine made of diamonds and pixie dust?"

I'm shooting the messenger. I don't care. My fury needs release, and this voice is what's in my way.

I slam the sign off button. My eyes fill with red. It takes me a moment to realize I'm pounding the dispensary. Adrenaline hides the pain. A desperate scream. My face looks ugly in the screen's reflection.

I awaken from my rage. My gun points at the machine. I'm officially crazy. I disengage the bullet before turning. People in the distance run away from my direction.

Sweat trickles my brow. Chest heaving. Hands shake. What the hell am I going to do?

- Chapter 19 -

I storm toward the Hub. The price of the new medicine haunts my mood. My mother is not telling me the whole story. I need the truth.

I burst in through the Hub's doors. The usual chatter fails to radiate in the lobby. A couple of Quentin's members casually travel between destinations, but nothing exciting. Part of me wishes Tony was looking for a fight. My fists would feed off him.

On top of the foyer, Vincent stands hanging over the ledge. His body leans forward. His glasses shine in the light. He pushes them up his nose.

"You finally show up." The look on his face says joke, but I'm in no mood for it.

"Can we make this quick?" I burst out while climbing the stairs. "I've got some money to make."

Vincent's smile disappears. He moves his hair to the side and crosses his arms. His eyes focus on my hands. They're bloody and torn.

I wince. The adrenaline rush is gone, and a sharp pain bounces off my knuckles.

Vincent's mouth opens. I raise my hands to halt his words, but he persists. "You know, Brock, you don't need to take on the world by yourself." He walks over to a first aid station and grabs medical supplies. "Clean up your hands and your attitude before you speak with Quentin."

My body tenses. Facing Quentin will only accentuate my mental exhaustion, the haunting memory of the last time I met Quentin upstairs. My body shivers.

Vincent helps me bandage my hands and then guides me through the door. I follow on the backs of his heels. My heart races when we approach the conference rooms. My mind fogs. Despite my destructive mood, I know it's valuable to heed Vincent's warning. As much as I hate to admit it, Quentin owns me. He made that quite apparent.

We approach the door that leads to the room where Quentin forced my hands into taking Jared's life. Quentin's invisible leash chokes around my neck. I think we're going to enter the room, but Vincent continues past it. My lungs release the breath, and along with it, the heavy guilt swelled up inside me. I shake my head as if that will prevent my mind from obsessing over the gruesome scene.

Vincent leads me two doors further down the hallway. He pushes the simple red buzzer. A small camera hanging above the door frame adjusts to our position. A click, and the lock unlatches.

The room is sizably smaller than I expected. There's a small round table that can seat about eight people located in the center of the room. Quentin and Tank sit in plush chairs facing the entryway. Along the far wall is an enormous screen. Underneath the large screen is a computer set up with a microphone.

Vincent tries to whisper something out of the corner of his mouth, but he's interrupted.

"Welcome," Quentin says and holds his arms up in the air as if he's about to accommodate my every need and ensure a comfortable stay. "I was informed you have valuable information for us. Please, sit down." Quentin says this as though we are old friends. His temperament is friendly, for now. I await the snake-ish lull and the venom to spew from his mouth.

Vincent and I take a seat. We sit across from the other two. Quentin's cane rests on the table.

"Start from the beginning," Quentin prompts. "Don't leave out any details." He leans forward placing his hands on his face with a silly grin like a child. A creepy, creepy child.

I inhale and gather my composure. I run through every event that happened the night before. Quentin prompts me with questions every now and then. His interest piques when I talk about the uniforms of the unidentified fighters. He wants to know the exact shades of gray, if there were any insignia that would provide identification, what types of weapons they used, did I see faces, and so on. I try to answer everything as best I can, but honestly, it was difficult to gather details with limited light.

Once I finish the story, Quentin stares at me for a few moments. His silly, childish grin disappears. His brow creases. He pounds his fists onto the table. "I don't like this," he finally says with hissing steam. "They sound too coordinated. Almost as if..."

"Pardon?" I respond. His reaction doesn't feel authentic.

With venom in his voice he says, "Don't interrupt me!"

His aggressive nature doesn't faze me. Not an ounce of respect towards him resides within my soul. This fear tactic to keep his mindless minions in line will not work. I'm not mindless, and I am not his minion. Right now, no fear.

My eyes fix into his. "I'm going to excuse myself." Vincent kicks me under the table, but I don't flinch, and my gaze dares Quentin. I have personal matters to attend to. I don't have time for Quentin to be off his rocker.

Quentin's face hardens. He looks like he's about to go ballistic. And then, as though a switch flips, he laughs. "Brock, you got balls. Big manly balls." He cups his hands out. "I like that about you."

Tank and Vincent nervously laugh. Quentin's laugh gains more steam. Everybody looks like they relaxed about twenty degrees. Quentin looks as though he's about to speak again, but within the blink of an eye, he moves, and he moves fast. He catches me off guard, and I feel a slight sting on my right arm. My eyes move to my arm and see my shirt is split open, and a surface cut shines red.

Quentin holds his cane out. A sharp object sticks out the bottom. He speaks through gritted teeth, "Just be careful of your fearlessness." This time his gaze sets me on edge, and I understand I should be fearful of this lunatic. He waves his hand. "You may leave."

I rise from my seat and look at Quentin as though I need his final approval. He waves at the air like I'm an annoying bug. My thoughts curse me. Why did I do that? My hesitation reinforces what little power I hold.

Before I leave, I catch a glimpse of Vincent's face. His face makes my heart hurt because I value his opinion.

I leave the Hub with only one thing on my mind, credits. My fighter's spirit will not allow me to remain stagnant and helpless. It's what I've always done.

In my apartment, I grab my drawings and venture toward the Forum. My disappointment rises. Most of my drawings sold the other day. I have no idea how I will get the medicine.

- Chapter 20 -

My entrance to the Forum is welcomed by my usual routine. Two drawings left. I grab my drawing supplies. Maybe an artist at work will draw customer attention. My mind goes back to early this morning when I saw the bird bringing her chicks breakfast. My hand makes fast flight across the canvas in an effort to capture the moment of peace.

The artist at work trick fails. It's a ghost town near me. I guess not every day can be like yesterday. The drawing joins my other work on the booth, and in that moment, I catch a glimpse of beauty. My heart skips a few beats, and my temperature rises. The beautiful girl wears a light purple dress patterned with white flowers. A thick white belt wraps around her waist. Her hair hangs straight and looks as smooth as her soft skin and glows like the moon on a dark night. She's stunning.

She's busy conducting business with other vendors. She turns and walks in the opposite direction of my booth. Sweat trickles down my skin. I wipe my brow and choke on the sandpaper feeling in my mouth. I'm going to do it. I'm going to approach her. Pep talk complete.

Abandoning my booth without worrying about my belongings, my feet fast track toward her. I don't want to draw attention by running toward her, but I'm practically speed walking. There are plenty of eyes on watch for criminals. If I look suspicious, I could be detained, or worse yet, shot by a guard.

I keep her in my vision. She stops at a fruit stand and examines an apple. This is my opportunity to close the distance. She talks with the seller, while spinning the apple around her palm. She and the seller laugh. Even through the din of voices, her laughter catches my ears. It's contagious and matches her smile. It's so full of life. Approaching from behind, I raise my hand to tap her on the shoulder, but I stall, and instead run my hand through my hair and turn away and pace a few steps. My hands shake, and my heartbeat pounds. I hyperventilate. My hearing goes numb. What's wrong with me?

I gather my composure. When I turn, she's gone. I do a full three-sixty scan, but in this part of the Forum, the crowd is so thick that my eyes cannot find her. That's when I catch the eyes of the fruit seller. I can tell by the funny look on his face he saw me wimp out. He points to my right and raises his eyebrows. The smile on his face spreads his thick mustache from cheek to cheek, and he whistles.

"Shut up," I say and move in the pointed direction. The fruit seller bellows a laugh as I leave.

Bobbing and weaving, I'm back on her trail. I accidentally bump into a few people on my tracking mission. All it'll take is one Pawn whistle blower and the guards will converge on me. Fortunately, no one seems to mind my belligerence.

My courage to speak with her steadily builds with each step. My pace quickens as though it is the final leg of a race. I'm about ten paces away when a group of three young men approach her. They're all blonde hair, blue eyed and walk with a swagger that says, "worship the ground we walk on." They look the same age as the girl. Her body tenses. I bend down and pretend to tie my boots.

"What a coincidence," says the one who appears to be the

leader of the group. "It's Lacey."

Lacey, what a befitting name for such beauty.

"Why don't you return any of my messages?" the same boy asks. "I'm starting to think you're trying to avoid me." He brushes the back of his hand along her hair like she is a prize.

Lacey bats his hand away in disgust. "Leave me alone Kyle. I'm not in the mood." Her face cringes.

"Looks like someone is a little touchy today." He turns to his two friends with a snicker and they laugh. "Is that any way to treat your boyfriend?" he asks with a smirk of arrogance.

Boyfriend? Another defeat.

Lacey sighs, "You're not my boyfriend. We went on one date. And, I might add, that I did it so you would quit pestering me."

"Let me remind you what you're missing." Kyle grabs hold of Lacey's face and pulls her in for a forced, ugly kiss.

Lacey's hands push on his chest, but Kyle tightens his grip. It lasts a good five seconds before he pulls away with that smug smirk.

Lacey's eyes light with fire. She snaps her right hand back, and slaps Kyle across the face. A red handprint forms.

Kyle's eyes lose their amusement and shift to anger. He grabs both her wrists hard enough she yells out in pain. "Listen here you little..."

It's time to make a move.

- Chapter 21 -

"That's no way to treat a lady," I say. I stand strong a few feet away.

Kyle gives me his attention and looks me up and down. His eyes stagger when he sees the prison garb. His smug swagger doesn't sway. "Who the hell is this? Move along. This is none of your business."

"I could, but I won't." My eyes dare him to approach.

Kyle releases his grip from Lacey and shoves her to the side. She falls to the ground. "Do I need to call the guards to send you back to the little doggie cage where you belong?"

I snort, "You would be a bitch and do that."

Kyle's eyes light like firestorms. He looks over at his two friends and says, "Looks like someone's asking for trouble."

My tactic works. Someone as arrogant as Kyle will not ignore me, even someone whom he thinks is below him. Kyle is a simple equation that's easy to solve.

"Kyle, please don't do anything," Lacey pleads.

"Oh, don't worry sweetheart, I'm just going to rough him up and we'll finish where we left off." He winks and blows a kiss. I nearly throw up in my mouth.

I look around the perimeter to observe the guards. No attention is drawn to us, yet. Whatever I do needs to be quick. This can jeopardize my sanctions in the Forum, but for some reason, I'm willing to do this for Lacey. She seems worth the risk.

Kyle walks up and stops six inches away standing eye to eye. Neither of us blink.

My taunts continue. "I recommend you walk away. I won't judge you."

Kyle laughs. "You talk a big game and now you want out?" He shrugs his shoulders, "You're nothing but a pathetic waste of space."

He pushes my chest, and I take one step back. I laugh inside. I wonder how he'd feel knowing I allowed his push? He won't stand a chance against me.

My lungs fill and release. "I'm going to give you one more warning. Walk away. If you decide to fight me, you'll get hurt."

Kyle looks back at his buddies and says, "Is he serious?" His gaze returns to me. "You think you're tough because you're a washed-up criminal?" He turns back to his buddies to get affirmation.

When he turns back around, a quick jab meets his face, just a little love tap to spark his anger. "First lesson of fighting, don't turn your back on your enemy."

He curses under his breath. His fists raise. His stance is so sloppy I almost feel like I'm about to beat up a child.

"I'm ready to kick your ass!" he shouts.

His words capture the attention of a few customers. The guards are still unaware of the event, but the crowd is noticing. It'll only be a matter of moments before everyone's aware.

He charges me. His first swing is slow. I simply sidestep and his momentum carries him off balance. He runs face first into a vendor booth. His head snaps back as he falls to the ground.

A small voice in my head warns me. I look around. A sizable group corrals in our direction. This situation is much more noticeable.

Kyle rises and looks defeated, but his pride settles him into his laughable fighting stance.

"You see," I begin to say, "your approach is too simple and predictable. You're never going to hit me like that."

Nerves hit again, Kyle roars in frustration. He charges; both arms flail like a windmill. He looks like a bad joke. I sidestep and dodge each attack with ease.

After a few seconds of ridiculousness, I decide to end it. On what I decide is his final swing, I catch his right hand and squeeze his fist until his bones squeal. His face contorts, and he crumbles to his knees.

"Have you had enough?" I ask. I squeeze harder, near the point before bones break.

"Okay, okay," he squeaks. "I'm done."

I keep ahold of his hand. "I want you to apologize to the lady and leave."

"Fine, just let go of my hand." He sounds like he's going to cry.

Shouts come from the crowd. I steal a glance at the guards and see them on their headsets and point. My time is about to expire.

I release my grip. Kyle shakes his hand and looks up with a face of hate. He walks toward Lacey and nods to his two friends.

Great, real subtle. The idiocy of this guy knows no bounds. I rotate my head. Looks like all three are going to get it.

Kyle turns around and on cue, his two friends follow him into their perilous assault.

With agile feet, I plant my boot in the center of Kyle's stomach. The wind releases from his lungs with a wheezing gasp. He collapses and writhes on the ground attempting to gasp for air.

Even if Kyle's friends wanted to stop their failed assault, my attack is too quick for them to change their momentum. The first friend meets a similar fate to Kyle's. A sweeping kick sends him flying in the air in a full three sixty before he faceplants. A cloud of dust hovers around his body.

At this point I notice the red dots. The guards have their sights on me. What's keeping me safe is how thick the crowd is. They must be reluctant to shoot for fear of hitting a Pawn. The guards shout through megaphones and demand people to move. The buzz of excitement keeps them watching and ignoring the commands. I'm glad I can provide them with pitiful entertainment.

I grab ahold of the next friend's shirt. My right fist cocks behind me. It wants my command. His eyes wide with fear.

My voice comes out a deadly whisper, "I gave a warning. I followed through on that promise. I'm going to tell you to do something, and if you don't, there will be consequences."

His Adam's apple bobs.

"You're going to gather these two idiots, leave, and never bother her again. If this doesn't happen, you'll be in a world of pain."

He looks down. I follow his eyes and see he wet himself. I let go and he quickly gathers his hurt companions.

That's when I realize I'm out in the open. My instincts send a tingle down my spine. I tuck and roll from my position, and as I do, a bullet hits the ground where I was standing. Shrieks from the spectators pierce the air. They finally understand the gravity of the situation.

I get down on my knees and put my hands behind my head. I hope the message is received. I wait for the impact of a bullet. Seconds feel like minutes. Nothing happens.

A booming voice barks orders behind me, "Keep your hands where we can see them and don't move."

I comply and feel handcuffs tighten around my wrists. I look up and see Lacey's eyes upon me. She runs in my direction.

"Let him go," she yells. "He was only protecting me."

One of the guards intercepts her advance. "Ma'am, stay

away from the criminal. We are following protocol."

"Oh, piss on your protocol," she fires back. She has spunk. "Is this how you treat a person who's protecting someone from bullies?"

"He's a prisoner."

"He's a person!" Her voice escalates.. "He's in the right."

She does her best to slip from his grip, but she cannot break his hold.

The guards haul me away in the opposite direction of Lacey when I hear her shout, "I'm the voice."

The voice?

"From the dispensary."

- Chapter 22 -

I shouldn't be surprised by how I'm escorted. Throughout the trip, I'm hit with the butts of guns, jabbed, kicked, and tripped. Each of the guards makes sure there's no second of silence. They fill my ears with derogatory names. Some of the things they call me don't even make sense. It's like they're trying to say every bad word in a string of nonsense. Normally, this would bother me, but one distinct thought floods my mind, knowing I can talk to Lacey again. I can't believe I didn't recognize her voice.

The guards drag me through an entrance that's near the exit to the Ashen Yard. We must be in one of the guard stations. Doors to different rooms create a line along a hallway, something I'm becoming familiar with. I get pushed along until we reach our destination.

"I got this one, boys," says the guard who handcuffed me. He removes his face plate, and a thin, cruel smile covers his face. "You," he points to one of the other guards, "Rookie, come with me. I'll show you how we do business." The other guards laugh.

We enter a bland room, like an interrogation room, but with no windows and only a chair placed in the center. Now the ramifications of my actions are clear. Nerves hit me. I doubt this will be my worst experience.

The guard sits me in the chair. A second set of cuffs strap on my wrists and are laced through the back of the chair. On the bottom legs, another set of cuffs secure around my feet. The chair is bolted to the floor. I squirm to act like I'm in protest. The guard smiles with pleasure. I let him have the satisfaction, but I'm really testing its strength. The bolts appear old and rusty.

"Now observe rookie," says the smug guard. He's old. His wrinkles fall to the ground. His nose is large, and I see bushes of white hair sticking out of his nostrils. With the way he looks at me, I imagine his predispositions. I bet his discrimination runs deep. That makes him dangerous.

He walks over to the younger guard and starts to speak in a soft voice. The rookie looks uncomfortable.

The older guard saunters over and pulls up his sleeves. He licks his lips like he's about to devour a savory meal. Once he's within a foot, he leans in. His face is within inches of mine. "You made a big mistake today you little maggot."

Ironically, his use of the word "maggot" fits perfect because his breath smells like something dead.

"Us honorable people from the Acropolis don't take kindly to filthy criminals who take arms against us," he continues. He keeps looking at my face as though he's analyzing my features. His evil laugh echoes off the walls. "Oh my god. You were trying to protect her. Is it because you fancy her? You actually think someone like her would want someone like you?"

His outburst surprises me. Despite being chained in front of these two, my thoughts should be on the moment, but I keep thinking about Lacey. My face must show it.

"Well, let me tell you. You will never, ever be with her. What do you have to say about that?"

He's like Quentin, trying to fester my anger. It subtly hits a nerve, but this guard is not worth the time. I act as though I think about his question. I finally respond, "When's your birthday?"

Now it's his turn to be surprised. "What the hell?" His voice rises with each word.

"I want to gift you a pair of nose trimmers. You could make a wig out of those bushes." My half smirk continues the message. No respect, even when he's in a position of power.

His face turns red. Steam could come out of his ears. "You're going to pay. I'm going to enjoy this." His look is hungry.

His right hand springs like a gun and propels toward my face. I brace for impact. When it comes, I tense my body and use my limited strength to rock back and forth. I hear the groan of metal, but nothing comes free. I'll need to work harder.

The sharp pain pierces my left cheek. My eyes water like a river. The impact of his hit is greater than I expected coming from an old man.

He knows the pain he inflicted. "That's right hotshot. Maybe you'll watch your tongue and show some respect."

His image blurs behind the curtain of tears. He winds up for a second attack. When the hit comes, I try to break through my restraints again. More squeaks groan from the metal, but again, nothing comes free.

My face throbs. I feel my pulse in my left cheek. Through a stream of tears, I observe the two guards arguing.

"Maybe you can't handle this job," says the old man. "Quit being a wimp and take a swing."

"I...I...," the rookie stutters.

"Oh my god, just get out of here. You're killing the mood."

The door opens and closes. I blink away the tears and see that it's only me and the old man.

"Kids today are soft," he says. "Now, where were we?" I hear his knuckles crack and his boots squeak.

Being a human punching bag is getting old. His fist winds back like a spring. I surge against my restraints and my right foot breaks free. It connects with the guard's groin, freezing his punch in midair. His hands fall to his injured bits, and he stumbles over with a breathy groan.

A portion of the chair's right leg broke free, leaving me unbalanced leaning forward, putting stress on the remaining bolts. I thrash like a wild animal rocking back and forth. The metal groans and the remaining bolts unhinge. The chair falls over. The side of my head bounces off the ground.

Both of my legs are free, but the handcuffs keep the chair bound to my back. I strain my imprisoned hands to break free, but it chokes my wrists.

The stifled guard staggers to his feet with a handgun held in his grasp. Colorful words fly from his mouth. Only feet away, he points his gun and shoots.

My instincts kick in. I turn and the chair provides some protection. My shoulders tighten and a stinging pain shoots through my right leg. Blood trickles down my leg. I can still fight.

The gunshots cease and more curses fill the air. I turn and see the guard attempting to reload his gun. My feet don't hesitate. The guard's eyes look my advance and his old fingers fumble with the magazine.

I plant my left leg on the ground and whip my right leg in a roundhouse kick. The sound of my foot meeting flesh vibrates off the walls. A direct hit to the left side of his face, redemption for what he did to me. The momentum carries his body toward the wall. Two thuds follow and the guard lies motionless.

The door opens and in comes the rookie along with a superior officer, both with their guns aimed. They look worried until they see the guard lying on the ground.

The superior officer chuckles, "Did you take him out while strapped to a chair?"

I shrug my shoulders and wince. My head pounds. Looking at my legs, a small streak of blood runs across my right thigh, thankfully just a bullet graze. With the adrenaline worn off, the pain trails up my body.

The guard looks at my leg, "I apologize, and we'll get you treated." He approaches. "I'm Lieutenant Roy, head of security." He tells me this like he's one of the good people. "We don't condone this treatment. Even though by law what you did was wrong, the young lady provided details of the situation."

His attention diverts to the rookie guard. "Why are you just standing around? Do you need help hauling that bag of bones out of here?"

"No, sir," the rookie replies. His voice shakes

"Well?"

The rookie grabs the guard from under the shoulders and hauls him out of the room.

Roy redirects to me. "I commend you for your valiance in the Forum. However, what happened cannot go unpunished. I'll be lenient." He pauses and looks at me like he expects praise. I remain silent. "Or I could not be lenient."

I better acknowledge his generosity. "Of course, thank you. A lot has happened."

My answer satisfies Roy. "Fair enough." He observes my head and leg. "Let's get you unstrapped and get you to some medical care."

My body tells me how much it hurts. Trying to force out of the restraints leaves bruises along my wrists and ankles. I try to walk without a limp, but I'm in terrible shape. My right leg hurts, my head is woozy, and my hands ache. Roy forces my arm around his neck and helps me walk into the hallway.

"This way to the Med Room," he says.

After we march a few paces, Roy asks, "By the way, how did you take him out?"

"Back me into a corner and I'll fight for my life," I reply. "That's what I've done my whole life, something I don't expect you to understand."

Roy laughs. "You're right. I don't understand. But I like your spirit. I hope I don't have to deal with any more Forum misgivings from you."

"No promises," I say back dryly.

Another laugh. "There's that spirit."

Roy opens the Med Room door, a sterile smell bombards my nose. Roy sets me down on a chair and speaks to the medical staff. He comes back with a warm smile.

"They'll take care of you," he says.

He holds out his hand. I hesitate. I've only shaken hands with Vincent once or twice in my life. I hold my hand out. Roy grabs it and squeezes hard. The gesture feels awkward.

"And by the way," he starts, "you chose the right person to protect. Anyone with the last name Pryce is a good person."

He exits the room.

Lacey Pryce. It seems fit that I learn more information about her because she already knows a lot about me.

- Chapter 23 -

I was wary of the treatment I'd receive. However, the doctor carries the same demeanor that as the lieutenant, Roy, showed me: genuine care for my well-being. Again, something I'm not used to seeing from Pawns.

"That's the final touch," says the doctor as he finishes patching my head. "The stitches will self-deteriorate. This ensures you won't be dependent upon another visit." He stops abruptly, like he planned on saying something else. Then he has a weird look.

"Thank you," I say breaking the awkward silence.

Roy enters the room.

The doctor removes his gloves, "He's ready."

Roy nods and snaps a pair of cuffs around my wrists. An ache pulses through my body. "Protocol," he says with a wry smile. "To make it look official." He escorts me out.

Roy strikes more conversation in the hallway. "Look, what happened today in the Forum doesn't look good on your record," his tone serious. "Normally an offense like this would suspend Forum activity for a minimum of six months. But after mine and Ms. Pryce's testimonies, they agreed to parole. You'll be assigned a guard you must stay within fifteen feet at all times."

It puzzles me by the fact this captain cares about my rights.

"Why do you even care?" My voice sounds harsher than I intend. I correct my tone. "I mean, nobody cares about the criminals."

He laughs. "I cannot say I fully understand. But there are people out there who want to help."

That is the extent of our conversation before he releases me back into the Ashen Yard. I gather my items from the Locker Room.

Even though I know the medical dispensary is powered down, I walk to it. I stare at the screen and see my reflection. My eyes glaze over, and Lacey's face glows from the screen. God, she's gorgeous. Those green eyes shining like pristine gems stare back at me. My heart pounds so hard I feel it in my ears. I want to talk to her. I'll come back first thing in the morning.

Back at my apartment building, dead silence creeps the air. The stillness of the evening hangs in the air like a fog. Before my hand reaches the doorknob, the door swings open and my mother gasps.

"Oh my god," she says as she hugs me tight. The pressure of the hug stings and sucks the breath from my lungs.

I push back. "Careful," my voice pained. My hand reaches for the side of my leg.

Fresh tears flow from my mother's eyes as she gives my body a formal observation. "What happened?" she asks me as she pulls me inside our apartment. "Are you hurt?"

I nod, "It's not a big deal. You know I can take care of myself." I regret the comment when I see the hurt in her eyes. I smile to try to lighten the mood.

My attempt fails. "Fine, I guess I shouldn't worry about the only thing I have in this condemned world." She walks over to the counter. "Here." She throws a sandwich on the table. "I'm sorry it's not fresh."

My guilt swells. "I'm sorry." I sit down and rub my eyes. "Someone was being harassed in the Forum. I stepped in to help. The harasser confronted me, and I did, well, you know."

She has a calculated look on her face. "What kind of trouble are you in? Was the person from the Acropolis?"

"Yes." My mother gasps, but I put up my hand. "Please don't feel sorry for me because I would gladly do it for her again any day."

My mother lightens up. "Her?" She sits down at the table and reaches for my hand. Her expecting eyes want the story.

My cheeks burn red. Again, it unnerves me to speak about a girl with my mother. She looks alive for the first time in a while.

A heavy breath escapes my mouth, "I saw the girl again in the Forum. The one I told you about last night. When I saw her, it was as if the world stood still and the only thing that mattered was her."

I continue the story about the events in the Forum. I don't go into much detail about the interrogation, or that Lacey is the person I speak with at the dispensary.

My mother tries to get me to talk more, but I express my exhaustion. She agrees I need some rest. We both head to our rooms for the night.

I try to fall asleep, but it eludes me. All I can think about is Lacey. No one's stuck in my mind like this. The clock says midnight. Why is this taking forever! What finally gets me to count sheep is reading a book.

When I wake up, it's still too early for the dispensary to be open. Being cooped up in the house sounds dreadful, so I gather everything I need, and head to the peace of my drawing spot.

I want to draw Lacey. I think about the moment I looked into her eyes in the Forum and felt time stop. I draw around the outside of the canvas, setting up the blurry Forum scene. This image captures what I saw and felt in that moment. It was like she was the only thing in the world. Lacey will be featured in the center. I realize I don't know how to approach her. Without color, her beauty will only be its shadow.

I take a different approach. She's still a mystery. We have a brief past, and she always shown me kindness. She would start casual conversations during our transactions at the dispensary. Even before I saw her, she made me vulnerable. Yesterday, I felt like she wanted me to see her. But why a lowly criminal? I shake off the thought and draw. Only half of her body is visible. The other half is cast in shadows. This is how I know her. I hope at some point I'll uncover what's hidden underneath.

When I finish drawing, I realize the medical dispensary will open shortly. I pack up and wander in that direction. What will I say? She told me she was the voice for a reason, right?

I'm at the kiosk, my heart a hammer, such an unfamiliar feeling.

A slight tremor runs through my hand as it approaches the commands of the kiosk. Come on Brock, get a grip. I stay calmer in life and death situations. This should be a piece of cake. Because of my nerves, I have to enter my code three times before I get it right.

"Who am I speaking with?"

I frown. The voice does not belong to Lacey, unless she recently became a man. Words fail my speech.

"Hello?" says the manly voice.

I sign off. A shockwave of disappointment. Disappointment is not unfamiliar to me. This time it feels different.

"What am I doing?" I question myself. How can I feel so defeated by someone I barely know? My mind wanders back to the comment of the old guard and his laughter. *'You actually think someone like her would want someone like you?'* How could I be so weak and stupid?

- Chapter 24 -

I storm to the Forum. I'll go crazy if my access is denied.

"Identification," the guard says in a gruff voice while holding out his hand.

I hand it over for his portable scanner. The red light illuminates the scan bar on my card, and the light on the scanner remains red. No access. The anger pounds inside.

"You've got to be kidding," I mutter.

The guard withdraws his gun. "You're a threat to law-abiding citizens. Exit this area or I will use any means necessary."

My irrational side wants to take the guard out, but my rational side knows that would be foolish. Trying to formulate a clever insult, my mouth opens when the other guard comes over.

"Wait," his voice rushed.

The guard with his gun pointed at me looks insulted by his companion's advance.

"Hand me your identification," says the second guard.

I look between the two until he gestures with his hand to hurry up. I hand it over, and he scans it. This time the color is orange.

"Just as I thought," he says. "He still has Forum privileges, but on restriction. I was told to look out for him." He pulls out a handheld device and taps the touch screen.

A rush of relief. At least I still have access to what little freedom I'm allowed.

"Why was I not informed, and why did my scanner have a different result?" asks the first.

"Don't worry," the second guard replies without his mask breaking contact from his handheld. After he finishes his business, his head raises. "There will be a guard who will survey your moves. You'll be under a microscope until the final investigation concludes from yesterday's events."

"Alright," I say.

The entrance to the Forum opens for me, and I release a relaxing breath. Now I need to figure out what I plan to accomplish here. A majority of the time I come here to sell my drawings. In the back of my mind, I know my true desire, but I don't want to admit it. I hang on the thread I will see Lacey.

"Hold it right there," says an aggressive voice.

Another guard. "Ah, you must be my shadow."

"As if I don't have anything better to do than follow the likes of you." It really is hit or miss whether someone is friendly or an asshole. This peach must've done something that pissed off his superiors to get stuck with this assignment. Either way, I'll have a little fun with it.

"We might as well become friends then," I say. "Want to grab a bite to eat?"

"Watch your tongue," he spits, "You're on thin ice."

I shake my head. "Yeah, yeah."

I walk without caring if my personal guard keeps pace. My feet direct me to my vendor booth out of habit. I'm about to change paths when I see someone standing at my booth. My heart jumps. Could it be her? They have their back to me and wear a dark blue hoodie. It appears they are writing something.

A rush of blood to my heart. The tremor returns. I can't

stand this onset anxiety.

When I am about two feet behind, I say, "May I help you?"

They startle, and when they do, I'm captivated. The dazzling gems flash and a bright smile follows. "It's you," Lacey says with genuine excitement.

Before I comprehend what's happening, she advances and intensely wraps her arms around my midsection. The hug activates the aches and pains littering my body.

There I am, standing with my arms strung out. I want to hug her back, but I feel incapable of returning the gesture.

"I didn't think I was going to see you," she whispers. There's a small tremble in her voice. "They are, um, giving me a week's leave from the dispensary. I didn't know if you would be able to come back in here because of what happened. I showed up with the hope," her voice fades, and she pulls back. "Thank you for yesterday."

When my voice finds its place, I finally muster, "You're welcome," although my voice sounds more like I am asking a question than a statement.

A voice behind us interrupts our moment. It's my new friend. "Excuse me ma'am, do you realize you're hugging a criminal?"

Lacey's eyes dart to the guard. "What's that supposed to mean?" she asks in a bout of hatred. "Do you have any idea what he did for me yesterday?"

"Well, the report says..."

She doesn't let him finish, "You can shove that report up your—" she doesn't finish the phrase, but the guard knows the intent. She huffs. "You don't even really care about what happened yesterday. None of you were there to help me when I needed it. All you care about is the fact Brock is a criminal, and not that he was trying to help me!" Her voice elevates with every sentence. Forum visitors look in our direction. "So yes, I know Brock is labeled a criminal. As if the way he is dressed wouldn't give it a way in the first place. Or are you insulting my intelligence?"

The guard steps back from the verbal assault and lifts his hands up in defeat, turning away from Lacey to avoid her burning eyes.

She whispers in my ear. "I have something I wanted to give you as a thank you."

Again, like the hug, I'm stupefied by what happens next. Before I can react, Lacey's lips connect with mine. She feels my body tense. She wraps her hands around my lower back like she's afraid I'll back away. Her eyes closed, the kiss is hungry, like she's been waiting to do this for a long time.

It takes me a few moments before I relax and settle into the kiss. Despite the intensity that sparks from Lacey, the kiss is tender. Her lips feel soft and warm with a subtle mint flavor. I've never kissed a girl before, but the experience is nothing short of heaven. I want the moment to live on longer

While Lacey pulls away, I feel something slip into my hand. "Here, I know you need this. Keep it out of view."

In my hand is a small round container. I reach into my bag and slide the container into a small compartment. I pull out my most recent drawing to help hide what I'm doing. I hand the picture to her. "This is for you."

"Is that me?" she asks.

My cheeks flush. "Yes, it was an attempt to get you off my mind, but it didn't work."

She places a hand upon my cheek. "That's so sweet." Her gaze drops to the drawing. "This is amazing. How can you capture so much beauty without any color?"

I try to think of something cool to say, but the only thing that escapes my mouth is, "Any picture with you in it is beautiful." The words nearly make me gag.

Lacey giggles and kisses me again. "I'm sorry, but I need to go. I know I'll see you soon."

- Chapter 25 -

I don't stay in the Forum after Lacey leaves. It feels like I'm a drug addict and got my fix.

The guard keeps to himself after the embarrassment from Lacey's barrage. His body language shows relief when he's released from his watch dog duties. I half salute him. "Have a wonderful day."

Back in the Ashen Yard, I dig into my bag and pull out the container that Lacey passed to me. Twisting the white cap, the lid pops off with ease. There's a folded piece of paper on top. I remove the paper and see little white pills inside. The tiny paper contains a phrase that reads, 'for your mom.' I pop the lid back on the container for fear I may lose the precious contents.

My excitement halts. Why is she doing this? Why is she going out of her way to help someone she barely knows? Would this put her in danger?

Her behavior toward me today is strange. She acted like she's known me a long time. The intensity of her kiss was fueled with desire. Not that I didn't enjoy every second, but the pieces don't add up.

I enter the apartment excited to tell my mother the good news. When I walk in, I hear nothing. I check the table for a note. No note. Before I let panic settle in, I pace down the hallway toward her bedroom. When I reach for the doorknob, a hacking sound reverberates from inside. It sounds like an exorcised demon.

Upon my entry, my mother lies on the bed with her body convulsing from the coughing attack. Small spatters of blood stain her lips.

"Oh lord," I muster. Without a second thought, I take off my shirt to use it as a towel.

She holds her hand up and points to a towel. I toss it to her. She covers her mouth and in a muffled voice says, "Don't come near me."

"You can't be serious," I gasp. "You obviously need help."

I proceed toward her, but she scoots to the other side of the bed. "Please, don't."

Frustration filters through my mind. "I need an explanation. What's going on?" My arms cross.

She struggles to catch her breath. After a few moments, she opens her mouth without coughing. "They say I have an autoimmune disease, nothing like they've witnessed. It's attacking my immune system. Pretty soon I will not be able to fight off infections." Tears well in her eyes. "They're calling it the Gray."

In a moment of silence, I reflect on her words. How's this possible? Why is this happening to my mother? "Why?" I ask

"They're calling it the Gray because hides behind its own cloud. It prevents the doctors from a proper diagnosis." The flood of emotions grabs her breath. "They don't know how anyone contracts it, possibly body fluids. Being air-born is ruled out since I'm the only known case."

This helps me understand why she keeps me away whenever she coughs. I curse under my breath. My mother is slowly dying. It's my turn for tears. Her words replay over and over. I won't accept this. She cannot be dying. I will not let her! Defeat brings me to my knees. If she's gone, truly gone, what will I become? She's the single bit of sanity I cling to. A piece of sanity that helps keep my bloody soul clean.

Lacey pops into my head. Why now? This isn't an appropriate time. While I wrestle with the thoughts that betray the moment, a laugh escapes from my mother and awakens me from my selfish thoughts. "Who knows? Maybe this Gray stuff is my secret weapon."

Leave it to my mother to turn a negative into a positive. Maybe this is karma for those dirty scumbags who use her. I have zero sympathy for the filthy bastards.

I remember the bottle from Lacey. "I have something for you." I run to the kitchen to get a glass of water. When I return, I set one white pill and the glass of water on the nightstand. "Take this."

She doesn't question my request and swallows the pill with a small sip. I set the bottle on the nightstand. She grabs it and reads the label. Her eyes expand. "Who gave this to you?"

I get down on my knees and prop my elbows up on her bed. "From Lacey, the girl I told you about from the Forum."

"I see. How did she get something like this? The doctor told me this medicine isn't out on the market yet, and it's still in development. It may be a breakthrough drug and only available to the most prominent citizens in the Acropolis." She pauses for effect. When I don't respond, she reemphasizes, "It's for the rich."

"Yeah, I know what you mean." I don't know how to process this information. "Let's just be thankful."

"Agreed."

"I'm going to let you get your rest."

My mother welcomes the thought and closes her eyes.

I walk out her room thinking about Lacey and the medicine. What is she doing? This adds to the puzzle pieces of her mystery.

- Chapter 26 -

Over the next couple of days, nothing major happens inside the Ashen Yard. I take care of my daily duties and visit the Forum to try and see Lacey. She doesn't make an appearance. The mystery continues.

Within a week, my restrictions within the Forum are lifted. There's no rhyme or reason. I didn't appreciate the old freedom in the Forum until it was taken away. It felt like invisible handcuffs were released from my wrists.

On my first day of reinstated freedom, Lacey makes an appearance. She meets me at my vendor booth, but this time, she carries a duffel bag.

Her eyes light up. "I'm so excited for today." She sets the bag on the ground and pulls her hair over her shoulders, a beautiful gesture.

I stand there clueless to her excitement. Lacey looks over her shoulder. "We are just going to need to find some place for you to change."

"Change? What am I changing into?"

She leans in and whispers, "Have you ever wanted to see what's on the outside?"

The outside? Does she mean the Acropolis? It's like Lacey can read my thoughts because she nods her head up and down.

"But how?" I query.

"You'll see."

Lacey holds the duffel bag in one hand and drags me with the other. My mind is consumed by how insane the notion of entering the Acropolis sounds. No matter what I change into, I'll never be able to pass through the security check point because I don't have proper identification, and, most obviously, my eyes, a dead giveaway. She takes me to a place where a mass of people crowd around the vendors.

She leans in to talk so she can be heard over the din. "We're waiting for a signal. In the meantime, I have two things for you." She reaches into a side pocket of the bag and pulls out two objects. There is a new ID card, but the second doesn't look familiar.

"Here you go," she says as she places the ID and the other object in my hand.

I look down to observe the unfamiliar object. It's a small container that has two circles connected to each other. Someone could fit a gumdrop in each circle. I open the container.

"Contacts," says Lacey. "Now your eyes won't get in the way, and there won't be any questions when you come to the Acropolis with me."

What's her plan? The thought of entering the Acropolis tantalizes me. Is this what Pawn children feel like when they open gifts on the holidays? It's exciting.

The uneasiness skyrockets to the surface, not because I'm worried about what happens to me, but what may happen to her. Harboring a prisoner is an act Pawns cannot turn a blind eye to.

My head shakes, "I'm not sure about this."

"What's the worst they are going to do to you, throw you in prison?"

"No, but they can throw you in prison."

Lacey pauses for a moment to gather her thoughts. When

she speaks, I expect an elaborate explanation, but all she says is, "It's worth it."

She opens the container, "Bend down like you are going to tie your shoelaces. When you put the contacts in, look up and to the side. That'll make it easier for you to slide them in."

I follow her commands. I fight the instinct to blink when my finger approaches. They're surprisingly easier to put in than I expect.

"Look into my eyes," Lacey prompts. "Let me see." I hold back for a moment and look into her eyes. "Look at those pretty blues." She playfully punches me on the shoulder. "You know, I'm not sure if I like the blue better than the gray. There's something about you and the color gray. With your art and your eyes, it seems to fit you."

I laugh. Thoughts of my mother filter through my mind because Lacey sounds like her. All thoughts converge toward my mother.

"Lacey?" I prompt.

"Yeah?"

"I can't stay. You know that, right?"

Lacey blinks a few times. "What do you mean?"

"I can't leave my mother alone."

She nods with a subtle flinch. "I expected it. I want to give you a taste of something beyond your life." She winks. Her confidence steady.

"Are you sure about this?" I ask. "Why are you risking so much for me?"

She leans into me and kisses my cheek. "You're so thoughtful. For the last time, don't worry about me."

She looks over her shoulder like she expects something to happen. She digs into the bag and pulls out a green t-shirt, khaki pants, and dark brown boots.

"When I get the signal, stoop behind this vendor booth." She points a couple feet to her left. "Change fast. Got it?"

I nod.

A loud crash and screams erupt a couple hundred feet away from us. Heads turn and the crowd moves in the direction of the crash.

"That's our signal," Lacey urges. "No one will pay attention."

At first, I don't move, instead my attention directs toward the commotion, but Lacey pushes me behind the booth. I strip out of my prison garb, and in less than a minute, I'm changed.

I reappear and Lacey scrunches her face, "Where are your other clothes?"

"Back there."

She throws her hands up in the air. "How are you going to get back into the Ashen Yard without your clothes?"

Her rationale is a blow to the stomach. Why didn't I think of that? I watch as Lacey enters the booth with her bag. She reemerges and grabs my hand. While she drags me to the gate of the Acropolis, we both make glances back toward the commotion. Guards swarm the scene, some people have fallen to the ground, mostly prisoners. The target of the guards is an Ashen Yard prisoner. He's acting like a lunatic. He looks familiar, and from what I remember, he never acted like that before.

We continue moving, and we hear a gunshot. We jump and look back toward the scene. The man is on the ground lifeless in a pool of blood.

Lacey mutters something under her breath. Before I can raise a question, we are in line with the other Pawns.

This is my first time participating in an evacuation when I wasn't lying on the ground. The guards keep the Pawns in a single file line checking for suspicious characters. This plan of Lacey's may actually work. My thought process changes when I hear the voice of the guard near the gate. It's a familiar voice–Roy.

In our approach, he squints like he's trying to figure out

what's in front of him. He recognizes me. My legs are stiff as boards. Roy helped me out earlier, for whatever reason, but allowing a criminal to walk into the Acropolis is vastly different than helping a criminal who is at the mercy of a guard.

Roy and I are face-to-face. A pause that feels like an eternity keeps us frozen in time. He breaks the pause and pats me on the back, "Enjoy." He winks.

I catch my breath. Lacey pulls me alongside her. We exit the large metal doors. For the first time in my life, I enter the Acropolis.

- Chapter 27 -

I cannot believe it. Never in my wildest dreams did I imagine I'd stand outside the walls of the Ashen Yard. As I take the moment in, Lacey calls for someone. A car pulls up. I notice an entire line of vehicles wait to take citizens to their destinations.

Lacey opens the door and we climb inside. This is my first experience inside a motor vehicle. My only experience with them is in books. The car is virtually silent. There isn't a steady rumble of the engine that I anticipated.

Lacey pulls a strap over her shoulder and inserts the metal end of the strap into a buckle. I follow her lead, fumbling awkwardly at first, but she grabs my hand and guides it.

The driver turns around and says, "Where to?"

Before she answers the driver, she looks at me, "Would you like to get a coffee?"

"Coffee?" I reply. "I've never had coffee before."

The driver coughs, "You've gotta be kidding? Anyone who's anyone has had coffee."

My cheeks redden. Mental note, don't sound out of place in the Acropolis.

Lacey shushes the driver. "Mind your business and take us downtown."

He touches the screen in the front. A timer starts and a

number of credits steadily increases.

My eyes attempt to translate the surroundings. One important note about the Acropolis is everything is clean. The drive is smooth, the roads are smooth, and there's no trash to be seen. Plenty of green vegetation tangles like webs along the walls of the freeway. Large green trees spread across the landscape like a sea of emerald. This place far exceeds my expectations.

I look at the towering skyscrapers. They're enormous and more magnificent the closer we get. Everything looks so sleek.

Within thirty minutes, we reach our destination. Lacey transfers the credits needed for the ride. My initial shock subsides, and the first thing I do is breathe in the air, so fresh. Everything about the Acropolis is pristine. It looks like someone took a giant brush and smoothed off every surface.

Lacey and I stand in front of a shop called the 4th Cup. Lacey looks at me expectantly, "Ready for a blast straight to your veins?" She laughs.

I scratch my head. "I guess."

When we enter, strong, yet intriguing aromas bombard my senses. The room radiates with a gentle buzz. I observe the beverages people drink. There's a split between people with a hot beverage with steam escaping from the tops of their cups, and cold beverages in clear plastic cups with ice floating on top. Every person fidgets with an electronic device, even the people who're having conversations.

Lacey guides me toward the front counter. A girl wearing a green apron and black hat greets us with a perky smile.

"What can I get started for ya?" she asks with a bounce to her voice. "Our specials are posted here." She points behind her head.

Lacey stands there with a finger touching her chin thinking. Once she orders, I understand why she was deep in thought. "I'll have an iced Venti, skinny, soy, caramel latte."

I stand there after the mouthful of words escape her lips.

Everything she said sounds like a foreign language. The worst part is the girl taking the order bobs her head up and down after every word without missing a beat while punching buttons on the register.

Once the girl finishes Lacey's order, she turns toward me expecting a similar mouthful of gibberish. I stand there, eyes wide, mouth open.

"Oh, I'm sorry," Lacey says. "He's never had coffee before."

The girl over the counter keeps her perky smile and says, "A first timer, huh? Welcome to the addiction."

"Do you have a favorite flavor, like chocolate or vanilla?" Lacey asks.

My head rattles. Water would do just fine I think.

"Chocolate," I reply. "Something simple."

"Iced or hot?"

"Iced?"

Lacey nods and orders, "He'll have a Tall Iced Mocha."

"Perfect," the girl replies. She punches the buttons on her register and Lacey pays.

A loud screeching sound makes me jump, a sound like someone's screaming. I glance behind the counter and see it's one of the machines used to make a drink.

"It's an espresso machine." Lacey grabs hold of my hand and squeezes affectionately.

Everything around me is so foreign. I could be in another country for all I know. I should be uncomfortable, but I love being with Lacey. Her soft touch brings chills up my spine.

Our order finishes and Lacey grabs the drinks. We take a seat at a small table.

Lacey stirs her drink for a moment before taking a small sip. She lets out a sound of satisfaction. "My favorite. How's yours?"

I look down at my drink. "I'm not sure."

"Come on, try it."

I take a sip. The taste is difficult to describe. The drink tastes chocolaty, but not in the sweet way I was expecting. Within a few seconds, I feel a buzz like I'm drinking liquid fuel. "Wow. This is different, but good."

Lacey laughs. "I'm glad you like it." She stirs her drink some more and looks at me. "Tell me about yourself. Who are you?"

The words surprise me. Talking about myself makes me uncomfortable. My mind travels back to the small encounters between Lacey and I at the dispensary. I revealed small pieces over the course of time, which was still too much for me.

I meet her eyes. "I think you know quite a bit already."

Lacey takes a small drink of her coffee. "I guess. Even if it came from medical records."

"That's invasive." My voice accusatory.

"Hey, look at where you are now." She points to our surroundings. "It got you here with me."

She reaches for my hand. I welcome her touch, comforting. I could get used to it. "Are you complaining?" she asks.

"Um, no." I lean in and my voice lowers to a whisper. "I was born in the prison."

It's her turn to lean in. "No, not that stuff. Tell me who you are."

My eyes lift to the ceiling. This makes my wheels spin. My thoughts produce a simple timeline such as being born there, never knowing my father, having a dying mother. This simple chronology doesn't answer the question, "who am I?" Now I ask myself the question.

I look at Lacey. My words falter and I look down at my drink. "I don't know."

Her expression softens. "I think you do know." She pauses. "Let me tell you what I see. I see a kind, considerate person. I mean, I always thought that because of how you take care of your mother. And then, what you did for me in the

Forum. You were so incredible. Oh, and your artwork! You capture intensity in the harsh gray lines, but the eye can see the gentle touch of care. I think your drawings are a reflection of you. At initial glance, someone may see a hard, rough exterior, but when they get in close, they experience a softness that bleeds compassion."

Her words hit me deep.

"You really are one of a kind." She gives me her heart melting smile. "I want to take you somewhere else. What have you ever done for fun?"

Fun? I'm not sure that word exists within my vocabulary.

Lacey guides me outside, drinks in hand. We walk at a casual pace, and I have a slight limp from my injured leg, but it does little to slow me down. People walk to their destinations carrying various bags, speaking on their phones, or thumb scrolling. Eye contact is a rarity. It's like everyone is trapped in their own personal tunnel. The steady hum from the vehicles creates a mesmerizing lullaby even as people race through the city. Horns are the sound of impatience. It feels like go, go, go.

My observations slow my pace. Lacey glances back and realizes she's a few paces ahead. "Why does everyone seem like they're in such a hurry?" I ask.

Lacey shrugs, "It's just the way it is here. I never really thought about it." She grabs my hand with a gentle pull. "We don't have much time. Keep up with me."

Lacey guides us through the busy streets of the downtown. She keeps a brisk, steady pace that I push myself to follow. My captivation of the city continues, whether it's the displays of neat clothing or gadgets in stores, or the nose guiding aromas of food. The aromas make my stomach yell, and I hold onto it, "I didn't realize how hungry I am."

"There will be food where we are going," she says. "Let's get you a snack in here." She points off to the side at a corner store. "I'll buy you one my favorite childhood snacks."

When we enter the store, Lacey looks at a small display underneath the front counter. "Here they are." She grabs two packages from a box. "These are mini chocolate cakes. These are my favorite, and I never get to eat them anymore."

My stomach growls again. This time Lacey can hear it. "This will hold you off before the Central Festival."

We're going to a festival? The excitement rises in my chest.

Lacey pays for the cakes. We are barely out the door before she rips the packaging off. "I can't wait for you to try this." Two little cakes slide out and she hands one to me. "Let me know what you think." Her smile giddy.

I take my first bite. A chocolate explosion bursts in my mouth mixed with a smooth creamy filling. My mouth tingles from the sweetness. My eyes close as I chew. This is delicious.

When I open my eyes, Lacey looks at me expectantly. "Well?"

My cake-filled mouth only allows one word to escape, "Amazing!" A small bit of cake launches out when I speak, and I place my hand over my mouth.

Lacey giggles. "I knew you'd like them. Now follow me."

I turn as I go in for my second bite. But my second bite doesn't happen because I collide with someone. My cake falls to the ground.

"Oh my god, who is the stupid idiot," says a semi-familiar voice.

Before I look at the perpetrator, I read Lacey, her eyes wide, frozen. I follow her gaze. Kyle.

- Chapter 28 -

"Look who it is," says Kyle. His hand brushes Lacey's hair.

His head turns my direction and my instincts take over. My hand forms in a fist and moves without thought. It comes around hard and connects across his face with a bone-crunching crack. Kyle doesn't know what hit him. He drops stone cold.

Lacey stands still like she's frozen with her mouth open. Her eyes dart from side to side. That's when I notice our surroundings. The atmosphere feels less rushed. Everyone who was just speed walking are now stopped and staring.

"We need to get out of here," she says and grabs my hand pulling us down the street.

I glance behind and see people holding their phones up. This isn't good. Lacey yanks me for a sharp right down an alley. Thirty-foot buildings scale up on either side of us. Our footsteps squish through the small puddles. We scale the metal steps running alongside the building.

"What're we doing?" I ask. My words come out breathy.

"Trying to make it difficult to find us," Lacey replies. She stops and looks. "Here we go." She pulls up on a window that is open by about three inches.

"This is crazy," I mutter under my breath. My mind questions Lacey. But who am I to question her actions when I

KO'd someone without a second thought?

We enter an apartment in what must be the main bedroom. Just as we enter inside the window, we hear voices from outside.

"Just in time," Lacey says. She looks around the room. Walking over to the closet, she opens it. "Here we go." She reaches inside and pulls out of couple of hats and tosses one my direction. She wraps her hair into a bun before placing the hat on her head.

Fortunately, nobody is home to catch us red handed. We shift our way through the neatly kept rooms. When we exit the front door Lacey says, "There's a skywalk on this floor."

In the hallway, Lacey looks both ways and moves to her right. "It's at this end."

We just make the corner when we hear, "Hey!"

"Keep moving," Lacey presses our pace.

We come to large glass doors that open automatically, and the skywalk Lacey mentioned passes over the street and connects to another building.

"Run!" Lacey shouts.

My heart pounds with stress and anxiety. We reach the other end of the skywalk with another set of glass doors automatically opening for us. Once we enter, we keep a brisk pace. She's smart, trying not to attract too much attention.

Inside the building, there is a large rectangular opening, and I can see all the way to the ground floor from where we are on the third floor. Scattered along the sides are shops.

"What is this place?" I ask.

"It's a mall. Sorry, we don't have time to shop right now."

"Wow, this makes the Forum look like a speck."

We blend in with the shoppers. Feeling safe within a small crowd, I finally look behind me. Men dressed in blue uniforms split up and search the area.

"The local law enforcement," Lacey whispers. "Let's keep a low profile."

Lacey surprises me and pulls me in for a kiss that carries some serious heat.

When we pull apart, I look at her and say, “Wow.”

She shrugs her shoulders. “Nothing makes people more uncomfortable than watching a couple have a make-out session. See.” She points. “They’re not headed this way.”

This girl has a strong head on her shoulders.

A group of people veer off toward a pair of silver doors. “Follow them to the elevator,” Lacey points.

The silver doors open. People file out and we file in. It reminds me of how the criminals of the Ashen Yard get into the Forum.

We descend to the bottom floor and exit with the others.

“I think we’re safe,” she says. “Now it’s time to get to the destination for our date.”

- Chapter 29 -

Lacey guides us to a central part of downtown to a large fenced off area. Inside are tents, rides, and other attractions. A neatly packed line of people await their entrance to the festival.

She wraps around my left arm and snuggles into me. "This is going to be so fun. My dad used to take me here when I was little."

Lacey's eyes look dreamy. This is the first time she's mentioned family. I take the opportunity to pry. Maybe I can balance the field of knowledge. "What's your dad like?"

"He's very busy these days." She directs my attention to one of the attractions. So much for leveling the field.

At the admissions gate, Lacey pays. The man behind the counter places a stamp of a red roller coaster on the backs of our hands. He secures an adhesive band around our wrists.

"What's with the wristband?" I query.

"It means we can ride as many rides as we want," she replies.

"Seems outdated."

"It's festive."

Lacey pulls me through the gate with anticipation. Once inside, she acts like a little schoolgirl. She reminisces about the times she came with her father. Our first destination is a place I kindly welcome, a small shack that sells foot long bacon wrapped corndogs.

I pull out my card to pay with what little amount of credits I own. Lacey blocks me. “I got it.” I feel defeated. Even though this is my first date, the chivalry protocol says the boy should take care of the girl. Maybe that’s outdated as well.

She holds both corndogs. It looks like she’s holding two weapons. My stomach growls.

Lacey speaks as we walk, “I didn’t mean to cut you off there. You need to save your credits for your mom, and I don’t want you to get tracked.”

Her words hit me like a ton of bricks. How could I’ve been so foolish? I’m usually aware of the cause and effects of my actions. I blame it on the new experience, but yell at my brain to return to my usual self-awareness.

We are still eating our corndogs when we pass by the dessert shacks. I get the message everything in this place is deep fried.

Lacey points to a another shack. “Before this date is over, you’ll have to try an elephant ear.”

“No offense, that sounds gross.” I scrunch my face to exaggerate my look of disgust.

Lacey playfully hits my arm. “Not a literal elephant ear. It’s dough shaped like an enormous ear, which is deep fried of course, spread with melted butter, and sprinkled with cinnamon and sugar. Every bite will melt in your mouth.”

I rub my hand around my stomach. “That does sound tasty. How are we going to burn off the mega dog so we can make room for one of those?”

“Come follow me,” Lacey beckons.

We roam around the festival. The lights illuminate the darkening sky. Lacey takes us through the different games, which are simple and rigged for us to lose, yet fun. The first game we play is a simple ring toss. The purpose is to toss rings around bottlenecks. Each bottleneck is a different size, making some easier than others to toss a ring around. The wider the bottleneck, the greater the prize. We test our tossing skills with little luck and move on.

We keep playing other games that include racing and other precision skills. The last game we walk up to is a shooting game. The contestants use a gun that shoots small pellets at targets that sporadically pop up. If there was any game that called upon my skills, this is the one.

"This is a childhood favorite of mine," Lacey says. "My dad and I always used to have competitions to see who could hit the most targets. Want to try it out?" She looks at me for a reaction. I don't give her one. "I'm pretty good. I bet you can't beat me."

I snort without thinking. "You can't be serious? I mean, come on."

"What's so funny?" She rests both hands on her waist. "Don't judge me because I'm a girl."

I hold my hands up. "Sorry. I didn't mean it that way. I just, well, you know."

"Lighten up." She giggles. She looks at the man behind the counter. "Two tickets. One for me and one for my boyfriend."

Boyfriend. The word rings inside my head. Reality sinks in. I smile. This dramatic turnaround in my life is surreal.

"What difficulty do you want to play?" the man behind the counter asks.

"Expert," replies Lacey.

The man gives her a look. "You know expert means a target will pop up every second for thirty seconds?"

Lacey glares at the man. "What's with men thinking girls can't do anything?"

The man quickly apologizes and sets the difficulty.

"Who goes first?" asks Lacey.

"Isn't the saying, ladies first?" I reply.

"So conventional. You nervous?" Her face says joke, but

there's a hint of seriousness.

Lacey grabs hold of the plastic gun. An air compressor hisses. The timer on top of the awning counts down: three, two, one. The tiny ding of a bell signals the start.

Targets of different shapes and sizes randomly appear from their hiding places. After the first five seconds, I understand Lacey is good. Target after target falls at the mercy of her accuracy. When the thirty seconds expires, she only misses two of the thirty targets.

Lacey hands the plastic gun to me with a smile and a hint of arrogance. "I guess I haven't lost my touch."

With a smug look on her face, letting her win will not be an option.

The timer ticks down. The small bell rings again and the targets slide into view. Even though the gun is plastic, it feels comfortable in my hands. My mind tunes out the world. My lifetime of survival transfers to this simple game. Even on expert difficulty, the targets feel slow. I claim all thirty. Lights flash and beeps sound around the booth as if I hit the jackpot.

I look over at Lacey. Her hands rest on her hips.

I shrug my shoulders. "I got lucky," I say with a smirk.

She laughs and hits my arm again. "What happened to being conventional?"

Apparently, very few achieve a perfect score on the expert level. I win a giant stuffed bear that's practically the size of me. We grab a ticket to claim it later.

"Do you get queasy?" she asks.

"Alright, are you doing this on purpose now?" I ask.

"Alright, Mr. Toughman. You may be able to beat me at a simple shooting game, but you're not going to keep up with me where we're going next."

Lacey guides us from the games to the rides. After a few rides, I understand why Lacey asked if I get queasy. I didn't know I was going to battle g-forces.

The ride that finally does me over swirls us back and forth.

We sit in a small pod. At first, she snuggles up next to me, but once the ride begins, our bodies are forced against each other by the constant change of direction. My stomach turns and I put my hand up to my mouth. Come on Brock, just make it to through this ride. I suppress the feeling long enough for the ride to stop.

When we get off the ride, it hits me again with a terrible tasting burp. “I need a trash can.”

“Oh no!” Lacey says. She walks me over to a can.

The contents of my stomach unload. I keep my head over the trash out of embarrassment.

Lacey rubs my back. “Are you alright, Mr. Toughman?”

“Yeah. The corndog tasted way better the first time.”

Lacey doubles over from laughter. “If you’re feeling up to it, there is one more ride I wouldn’t mind going on. Don’t worry, it’s easy going.”

I reply with my head still in the trashcan, “Well, I don’t think there is anything else that can come up.” I rise from the trash and rub my shirt across my mouth. “One more won’t be so bad.”

“Let’s get something to drink first so you can clean your mouth,” says Lacey.

Grabbing sodas, we enjoy the refreshing drink. I use the first sips like a mouth wash. The fizzle and pop of the citrus soda helps flush my mouth and then finish the bottle.

We approach our final ride and my heart hammers against my chest. The name of the ride is called “The Tunnel of Love.”

A range of couples young and old wait in line for the ride that claims it’s meant for passion. We watch couples get into pink, heart-shaped boats that venture down a makeshift river and disappear into a tunnel. The closer we get, the more my heart beats in anticipation. Just a few days ago, Lacey appeared to be a distant woman whose beauty caught my attention. I never imagined I’d go on a date with her. Now she's referring to me as her boyfriend.

We reach the front of the line. The little boat docks and parks awaiting its next guests. Lacey looks at me. Her face blushes.

I take hold of her hand, like a gentleman, and guide her into her seat. I settle next to her.

The ride attendant pulls a bar across our laps. "Enjoy the Tunnel of Love," he says as he pushes a button engaging the boat's track.

The instant drop of temperature feels fresh. We are consumed by the dark tunnel.

The inside of the tunnel simulates an enhanced water ride through Venice, Italy. An Italian man's strong voice sings a melodic song that's rich and comforting. Warm, soft lights luminate from different light fixtures that look like lamps and candles. Lined up along the tunnel walls are artistic buildings, some of which have mechanized people acting out scenes. One scene shows a man down on one knee pleading at the bottom of a building. A woman stands on the top balcony with arms folded and a disapproving look. I play out what the man did to beg for forgiveness, but it makes me think of my mother and her jobs. I shutdown the thought.

Lacey interlaces her fingers into mine, bringing me back to the moment. I turn my head and see her sigh as she glances around at the scenery.

She leans her head against my shoulder. "This is perfect. When I'm around you, I feel like a different person. You're so gentle and kind."

I linger on her words. I wonder if she'd feel the same if she witnessed my past or what I do on a daily basis. She expresses her feelings to someone whom she cannot be with. Even in this moment of bliss, I understand what we're doing is forbidden. How long will this last? I shove the thoughts away. Just enjoy, Brock, stop spoiling the moment.

I squeeze her hand. "I feel the same way. You make me

feel like a different person. This is one of the best days of my life. I want, I wish I could see you every day."

Lacey raises her head from my shoulder and gazes into my eyes. "It's up to us you know."

I scoff. "I wish it were true, but there are major roadblocks in the way."

She attempts to respond, but I do not let her. I make my move and tenderly kiss her. She kisses back. Time freezes. Her soft lips encourage the feelings I have for her. Unlike our other kisses, this one doesn't take me by surprise. The sudden rush of emotions makes me dizzy.

When we split apart, Lacey smiles and her eyes gleam. She leans her head on my shoulder again. Throughout the rest of the ride, we sit and enjoy it. My heart hammers in my chest.

After the ride, Lacey and I go to the vendor selling the elephant ears. She purchases one to share and walks me to a grassy hill near the edge of the festival.

"They have fireworks tonight," she says. "This is a good spot to watch."

We split the delicious treat and the fireworks begin. The two of us lie down on the grass holding hands and enjoying the fireworks that illuminate the sky.

"I could lay here all night," Lacey says. "I want the world to stop."

Her words ring true. I feel as though we're living in a dream. A dream I'll have to awaken from and return to my harsh reality.

The fireworks conclude and Lacey remembers to collect the massive teddy bear before we leave. We pick it up and lug it out of the festival gates. Lacey calls for a ride. As a joke, we seatbelt the bear into the backseat and make it gaze out the window.

I notice the time. There's no way I'll be able to return to the Ashen Yard this late at night. Lacey grabs my hand as though she's reading my mind. "I've got ya covered."

I have no reason not to trust her. She has already gotten me this far.

- Chapter 30 -

Sure enough, Lacey gets me into the Ashen Yard. Just like when I left the Forum and entered the Acropolis, Roy acts as though there's nothing suspicious about a criminal wandering the Forum after hours. He personally escorts me and pats me on the back before parting ways. The pieces of the puzzle aren't connecting.

I walk back to my apartment in complete bliss. This feels like a new beginning. A new me I never thought possible. My hard exterior cracked. I used to consider that a weakness, but I question my old way of thinking. Being with Lacey is like reading one of my books. I become lost in a world I never thought possible.

I approach the steps to my apartment still lost in my daydream. I want to avoid giving a name to these emotions I feel, but I give in and recognize I'm in love. The only other person in my life I've felt love for is my mother. Obviously, this feeling is different. The softness of Lacey's touch and the warmth of her presence make me feel like an actual human. Not only has love cracked my hard shell, but it's filling me with another unfamiliar emotion, hope.

One step. Two steps to the top. Reality slaps me when the front door hangs ajar. I tense and reach for my side. Of course, I don't have my guns.

Peering inside, I'm greeted by darkness. It feels like an eerie cloud lies in wait. The only sound comes from my shallow breathing. I reach around the corner where my utility belt hangs inside the doorway. Nothing. Senses kick into overdrive. Tiptoeing across the kitchen, I grab one of the large knives from the counter.

"Mother?" I call in a worried voice. "Are you home?"

Silence answers my call. Creeping along, I stop. In the middle of the hallway, broken glass from the mirror paints the floor. The gut wrenching feeling of my mother taken hits me.

I notice the door to my bedroom is not closed. Someone's been inside. I walk toward my room determined to find out what happened.

I stop a few feet away. One, two, three, kick! With a bit too much force, the door flies open as I burst in with my knife extended. Quentin holds my mother, who's gagged and out cold. He points his gun in my direction. I hear clicks from behind. I'm surrounded and outnumbered.

"I see you're finally back," Quentin says. "I'm glad you didn't take too long. It appears you had quite the little adventure. Now drop the knife. You look pathetic." He laughs.

"What have you done with my mother?" I hiss.

"Whoa, slow down there, tiger," Quentin coos. "Where are your manners? This will not do; this will not do." Quentin shakes his head back and forth. "You know Brock, after everything I've done for you."

I try to cool my rising temper. "What do you want?"

"This is not the time and place to talk about it," he replies. He gives an affirming nod to someone behind me.

The next thing I know a great pain fills the back of my head, and darkness blankets me.

- Chapter 31 -

My head screams, an unmerciful pounding drums from the back of my head to my temple. I want to feel the back of my head, but my hands are constrained behind me. My mouth is gagged and a blindfold keeps my vision dark.

I use my nose and ears to gather information. The air smells moist and musty. I hear a muffled whine coming from about ten feet in front of me. The noise sounds female, and I assume it's coming from my mother.

My muscles test the strength of the restraints pinning me to the chair. One thing is clear, they don't want me to move. My movements snap the attention of our captor.

"He wakes," says a deep voice and the infamous sound of knuckles crack.

"Remove the blindfold and gag," says another voice. There's no doubt the voice belongs to Vincent. "I'm going to inform Quentin our little handful is awake."

Tank laughs and his rough, strong hands remove the gag and blindfold. He makes sure and gets a few jabs as he removes them. Cowardly.

I gather my bearings and look around. I'm in a darkened room that appears underground because there are no windows and the temperature is cool. In front of me sits my mother still bound and gagged. There doesn't appear to be any injuries on here. A small victory.

Vincent and Quentin enter the room. Quentin's eye has his classic psychotic twinkle. It's magnified by the twitch of his eyelid. Both ugly features are a sign of irritation. I'm certain he knows about my venture into the Acropolis. Capturing me is not what worries me. It's the fact my mother is involved. I can handle what they throw at me, but my mother is frail.

"What're you doing?" I seethe. "What's the meaning of this?"

"Quiet," Quentin screams. "I'm not putting up with your insubordination. You don't have the authority to ask questions. Do you understand?"

I sit there and glower at Quentin instead. I want to show Quentin I'm not afraid.

"I see you don't quite understand," he says.

With that, he nods at Tank. Tank walks over to me and punches my gut with enough force to break bones. The air siphons from my lungs, and it takes me a minute to regain my composure. I glare up at my opponents and show a face devoid of respect. Message sent.

"You still don't understand," Quentin says with more malice. He nods at Tank again.

Instead of heading in my direction, Tank walks to my mother.

"No, wait," my voice desperate.

He takes out her gag. Before she can say anything, Tank institutes the same punch he applied to me. A weakened cry escapes my mother's mouth. Tank returns the gag to quiet her cries.

"You bastard!" I yell at Quentin. My body tries to move but to no avail.

"Wow, you would think he'd learn," Quentin says to Vincent. "Maybe he still doesn't take me seriously."

Tank steps aside as Vincent moves. He takes a knife from his waistband. My mother's eyes pulse with fear. Faint whimpers escape the cloth gag. Vincent slides the sharp blade along the side of her arm, leaving a thin red line. Blood slowly trickles down her arm, almost artistically. More whimpers and tears come from my mother.

Vincent looks over at me. His eyes send me a message, a message to cooperate.

I think of the terrible things I want to do to the three of them, but admit defeat, and sag in the chair. "What do you want?" I ask.

Quentin boos, "Why did you come to your senses? I was hoping we'd get a bit more blade carving before your submission." His look twisted.

He sighs, "I digress. Tony!" he screams up the stairway.

Tony emerges from a set of stairs to my left. His chest puffs out. "Yes sir!" he says a little too enthusiastically.

"You issued a small report to me yesterday," says Quentin. "Summarize it."

Tony has a victory grin like he finally beat me in the Ring. "I noticed Brock speaking with a Pawn in the Forum." Tony glances at me, eyes smiling, "I have to say, I was surprised someone that pretty kissed someone pathetic like you."

Quentin waves his hand. "Enough with the theatrics. Get to the meat."

Tony regains his composure. "While I was roaming about yesterday, I noticed someone who looked a lot like Brock dressed in a Pawn's clothes. It didn't take long for me to identify the person as Brock with the pretty girl going toward the Acropolis, while people like me were lying on the ground with our hands behind our head."

Tony looks at Quentin waiting for praise. Quentin gazes at Tony without a change of expression. After a few seconds, Tony gets nervous and asks, "I did good, right?"

Quentin rolls his eyes, "Oh my god, does everyone need my affirmations? Yes, you idiot."

Tony's moment of victory is soured. He stands still looking

like an idiot.

"Quit standing there like that. It's creepy." An interesting comment coming the king of creep.

Tony salutes and leaves. Before he's out of sight, he turns and flips me the finger.

Quentin raises an eyebrow. "Interesting report. Now I'm only going to ask this once, and I expect to hear the truth." Quentin pulls his handgun from his waist and points it at my mother.

Inexplicable fear blazes in her eyes. I beat myself up for being so selfish. I didn't think my actions would impact the most loving person I know.

This time without a second thought I confirm the truth to Quentin. "It's true."

"I'm glad you are cooperating," Quentin says. He points the gun at me and fires. I feel the bullet skim my left cheek.

The breath holds still in the room. It happened so fast.

"Oops," Quentin laughs. He raises his shoulders, "It slipped."

Adrenaline rushes through my body. My heart beat drums in my ears. I already knew it, but damn, this guy is crazy.

"Now I want you to listen very carefully," Quentin says as he approaches me with a swagger that does not match his age. "First of all, this place doesn't have an open-door policy where you can come and go as you please." He grabs a hold of my chin with his hand. His face is only inches from mine. I smell fish on his breath, and I nearly gag. "You are my property. I own you. You come when I call. You come when I don't call. When I need you to fight for me, you will be there. Do I make myself clear?"

I nod.

Quentin releases my chin. "Good, I'm glad we cleared that up. You don't need to make things so difficult. Here's an example for you, don't try to get into the Forum. Your days there are over."

I try to remain confident, but he cracked my armor, and I'm losing the battle.

Quentin gives me one last smug look and turns toward the exit. Before he leaves, he turns around. "Oh yeah, I forgot one tiny thing."

He looks at my mother and says, "You know I really hate doing this. But I feel it's necessary." Like the first shot, it happens so fast. The bullet escapes from the mouth of the weapon. It's followed by the terrifying scream bursting from my mother.

On the arm opposite of the cut, blood oozes out.

Quentin laughs. I fight the urge to scream at him. Everything is my fault.

Quentin smiles like a child. "Good boy." He looks at Vincent, "Get her patched up."

Vincent abides Quentin's orders and takes her out of the room.

Quentin directs toward Tank. "Do the final part. Don't be too hard. I still need him in battle shape."

Tank cracks his knuckles, and it sounds like booming thunder. "Ya gots it." He looks happy. "This goin be fun." He licks his lips.

Tank hulks over me. His smile stretches from ear to ear. "Aight kid, this only gonna hurt – a little."

The last thing I remember is Tank's enormous fist hurtling toward my face.

- Chapter 32 -

Aches. Stiffness. Streaks of pain. My eyes aren't even open when I'm consciously aware my body's condition. My nose picks up the scent of the small comforts of home. I stir on the soft surface. Covered in blankets, I feel warm and almost peaceful.

Every part of my body feels heavy like stones arc attached making gravity my cruel enemy. It takes a few moments for my eyes to muster the energy to peel open. When they finally do, the familiar scene of my room fills my vision. Everything appears normal.

Taking a deep breath, I lie in my bed recounting the details before I lost consciousness. I remember Tony tracked me inside the Forum and reported to Quentin.

It hits me. There will be no more visits to the Forum. I'm certain Quentin already pulled the strings. That means I won't be able to see Lacey. The realization is jarring, especially coming immediately after the most incredible evening of my life. I try to talk myself down. Who am I kidding? How long did I really think my relationship with Lacey was going to last? I should be happy with what I got. An opportunity presented itself, and I took advantage. What's the saying? It's better to love and lost than to never love at all. Not convincing.

A pang of guilt slaps me. After all that happened, I wake up, and my first thoughts are to feel sorry for myself. My first thoughts should be about my mother. When I'm supposed to protect her, I caused her pain. The guilt and shame roll up around my body, suffocating my mind.

These thoughts are enough to set aside the pain and force my body to move. Painstakingly slow, I roll out of bed. My face contorts associated with Tank's beat down. Fortunately, none of my bones feel broken.

I move to my dresser mirror before I leave my room. I look into my gray eyes. Sagging bags that days of sleep couldn't cure sink downward. A small canvas of bruises and cuts reveal my conflict. I've looked better. I feel worthless as it is.

Walking out of my bedroom, I limp down the hallway toward my mother's room. I hear a clanging noise from the kitchen and change direction.

I enter and my mother sits at the table stirring hot tea. She looks up. I soak in the details of her injuries. They're similar to mine with hills for bruises. Where she's got cut and shot are white bandages wrapped around both arms with dark red bloodstains.

I take the seat across from her. "I'm so sorry I did this to you." My right leg bounces underneath the table.

She looks at me with her soft gray eyes and musters a smile through the pain. "Don't apologize. You did nothing." She takes a small sip of tea and tears well up in her eyes.

Frustrated, I shake my head. "Are you serious? I mean, look at you. You were on the wrong end of a knife and a gun. All because I was so damn selfish because I got to experience life outside of here. With her." I rub my eyes to help relieve the hounding pain pulsing in my head.

I hear a painful laugh. "Experience life with her, huh? I assume you mean Lacey. I need something to brighten my day." I open my eyes and her face prompts for details.

I turn my head, and laugh in embarrassment. I clutch my side and catch my breath. My face feels warm.

"How about this," my mother begins. "Instead of dwelling on the terrible things, how about you tell me about life with Lacey?" She nudges me with her hand.

Looking at her, so eager, I have no choice but to tell her about my date.

I talk about the festival. I envision the place in my head and try to capture the looks, feels and smells of the place. My mother salivates a little when I talk about the deep fried, bacon wrapped corndog. I move on to the shooting game. This is the part of the story she gets a kick out of. She teases me about how I let my pride get in the way by denying Lacey the victory.

Throughout the story my mother laughs and prompts with clarifying questions, yearning for details. Seeing her laugh and smile is the therapy I need to help heal my tormenting guilt.

I blush and grin as I get to the Tunnel of Love.

"This'll be good," she says without trying to contain her excitement.

My eyes grind in a heavy roll. "Calm down," I tease. "The Tunnel of Love is this little water ride. They have these heart shaped boats that seat two people."

"How cute," she interjects.

My voice quickens. "Anyway, there were puppet-like characters acting out scenes. Lacey held my hand and leaned her head on my shoulder. And yes, I know you are going to ask this, so I'm going to spare you the breath. We kissed."

"You're healing my wounds. You're reminding me of my days with your father." Her eyes wander off into the distance.

"Did you two ever go on dates?"

This catches her off-guard. "Oh, I suppose. There's only so much you can do in a place like this." Her eyes light up. "There was this one time, oh your father, he was so sweet. He packed food up in a basket. He left me a note that told me to meet him at 'our spot,'" she does little air quotes when she says it, "just before sunset. The spot in his note is a place with three large evergreens near the apartment."

After hearing those last three words, it hits me. She's talking about my drawing spot.

Her voice awakes me from the thought. "We had this small meal and watched the different shades of orange glow in the sky before the stars came out. We laid on our backs and watched the night sky. I remember lying there and wishing we could freeze ourselves in that moment."

Goosebumps form. "I had that feeling last night."

"Does that mean you're in love?"

It takes me a moment to think about her question. That's what I felt yesterday, but now I attempt to be logical. There's definitely something there. Something I've never felt before. My eyes scan my mother's injuries, and it's enough to sober me the thoughts of love.

I redirect. "You look like you're doing better. I mean, besides what happened yesterday. Your face has more color."

"I feel the best I've felt in a long time. Whatever you got sure is the magic pill."

Seeing my mother feel better hits me with a gut-wrenching realization. Because of Quentin, not only will I not see Lacey, but there's no way I'll get medicine any time soon. "Do you think the medicine is something you only need to temporarily take, or is it a long-term drug?"

My mother shrugs her shoulders, "I have no idea."

The thought unsettles me. "I feel like I'm stuck between a rock and a hard place. My life changed and provided me with an incredible experience. Quentin will no doubt sabotage that."

"I understand," she says.

"Excuse me for a moment." I head into my bedroom and grab my bag of art supplies. I walk back into the kitchen and hold up my bag. "Therapy."

My mother nods as I head toward the door. Her voice holds me up. "I'm sorry."

"Why do you keep apologizing?" She's about to speak, but now it is my turn to interject, "I need to unwind."

I head to my spot, formally my parents'. When I sit down, I run my hand across the grass as if I'm trying to feel a memory. Listening to my mother talk about my father always makes her face shine. A happiness that is a distant memory. I finally understand that happiness. It's a warm hug on a cold day. My mother clings to these memories, this happiness.

My thoughts shift from a cozy memory to defeat. As much as I try to be her protector, her confidence, her caretaker, she'll never regain that happiness she felt when my father was alive.

My thoughts transition to anger, and I'm surprised. I should be angry with Quentin or myself, but my anger makes a pit stop at my father. He's selfish. How could he abandon his wife and child? I've survived this place for eighteen hell-ridden years. He could've stayed. He was weak.

Before I realize it, my hand glides across the canvas. My strokes are fierce. I gather in the details. The setting is a top-down view of my current location. The contours are of a young boy and girl. They're caught in a moment of bliss gazing up into the sky, consumed by a world that is intangible. Looming behind them hulks a sinister shadow. The couple is blinded by their own feelings. They cannot see the message hidden in the shadow. They are doomed.

I look closer at my work. The setting is ambiguous. It may or may not be the spot where I sit. The faces of the young couple are not clearly defined. My drawing tells the story of my parents', or my own doomed relationship with Lacey. Neither story has a happy ending.

- Chapter 33 -

Nothing exciting happens over the next couple of days. Instead of heading to school, I stay home and rest. I wait for someone to come and get me, but nobody bothers. Quentin must feel like he's still in control and not worried about my absence.

Lying on my bed, I recount the recent events. Before the past week, I understood my life. I'm a born criminal residing in the Ashen Yard. I joined Quentin's gang the day of my thirteenth birthday. I'm an effective member of the gang, one of his most lethal. I carried out orders as I was told. I kept my humanity by educating myself through reading and kept my emotions in check through drawing. Then came the temptation of seeing what was beyond the walls. I reached for the forbidden fruit, acquiring a small taste. Now that I have a taste, I don't want this life anymore. Nothing feels the same.

While I lie down, a depressing laugh bursts from my mouth. It's not as sinister as my outburst after Jared. It feels defensive.

My mother walks in after my outburst. "Is everything alright?" She received medical treatment for her laceration and bullet wound. It didn't take long for her to bounce back.

I dismiss her concern. "Yeah. How're you feeling?" Even though she appears in good health, concern runs its course because she took the last of the medicine yesterday.

She looks up and down her body. "I feel the same. We may need to wait a few days."

"I'm going to go to school today," I declare. My mother looks confused. My eyes roll as I say, "I'm sure Quentin has been so gracious to allow my rest. We both know this respite isn't going to last forever. I need to show my face so there isn't any more collateral damage."

From the look on her face, she knows what I mean. Her voice comes out strong, "It's been nice having you around the past few days. It actually felt like a normal life. I don't want you to get hurt anymore."

"The same goes for you. Look, I've played this game long enough. I pushed the boundaries. I will not turn into a mindless thug of Quentin's. I can think for myself, and you know that."

Rising from my bed, I give her a hug and pull back, "Trust me."

A single tear slides down her cheek. I attempt to reassure her with a smile before kissing her cheek. I grab my gear, and exit the apartment.

Walking toward the Hub, I think of Lacey. As much as I wish I could forget her, she's stamped on my heart. I wonder what she's doing right now? Is she thinking about me as much as I'm thinking about her?

I reach the Hub and get scanned in. The main entry is empty. The early morning lectures are finished, so everyone is in their combat sessions. I look at the time and see it's ten o'clock. I head toward the Ring and see my group readying for hand-to-hand combat. I want this. My energy levels are high. My bumps and bruises breathe no pain. There's so much high-strung tension bound tight in my body. I cannot wait to release it. I feel dangerous. I know exactly who I'm going to take it out on.

I change in the locker room and enter the Ring. My

presence is noticed immediately. The first person I make eye contact with is Tony. He looks my way, and his face twitches. The next person I look at is Vincent who looks confused.

"You're not ready to fight," Vincent says to me.

"You think being tied to a chair and getting pummeled is going to slow me down?" I seethe. I stretch and show my limber body even after getting beat up. "Besides, I need to give Tony a little message. From my fist." My eyes burn with determination.

Tony can't look at me. "Sorry to disappoint you, but I already have a partner."

My voice elevates to a shout and everyone freezes. "Hey, look at my face!" He looks at me and I continue, "Do I look like I care? You were already a little bitch once. You going to be one again?" I wave my hand at my rhetorical question. "You will fight me, and I will destroy you." My eyes, the devil's, meant to light fire to his skin.

My taunting words punch Tony. He attempts to bring his confidence in front of everyone, but doubt treads in his words. "Let's do this lover boy."

Snickers from the group fuels my determination. Looks like he decided to share his story with everyone. The fire inside smolders.

I jump into the center ring. "I know you're scared, but don't keep me waiting." Everyone fidgets with anticipation. My face turns hard as stone, and even in the stillness of my stare, a terrifying thirst burns.

Vincent interjects, "Your fight is slated last. Besides, you shouldn't be fighting so soon."

"Shut up, Vincent." My stare turns to him. When I look, the replay of his knife sliding along my mother's arm burns deep. I want to smash his face in along with Tony's.

My insubordination stuns silence amongst everyone in the Ring. Surprisingly, Vincent doesn't respond and stands ready to referee.

Tony enters. Since day one, he's hated me. It's my turn to return the hatred. Rage festers in the bottom of my stomach. Rage from the terrible life I live. Rage from Quentin who makes me kill. Rage from the fact I cannot be with Lacey. Rage for my future victim standing across me.

We both prep and meet in the center. Tony holds out his fists to get bumped. I refuse to return the gesture. I maintain the terrifying gaze of determination. Tony's unnerved. He looks like a little kid. A kid who wishes his mommy could hold him and tell him everything will be alright. It will not.

Vincent starts to say the guidelines, but I interject, "Just call the fight."

He has a calculated look. I'm not sure how much longer he'll let me hold this attitude.

Vincent initiates the fight. Tony takes a few steps back and holds his fists up ready for my charge. I don't move. I don't get into a fighting position. I stand in the center with my arms hanging at my sides.

Tony bounces around in a state of confusion. The initial wave of shouts from the spectators fills the room, but the more I stand still, the quieter they get.

Tony pretends to charge. He stops short by a few steps and retreats back. Not a muscle in my body moves. My vision tunnels to only his face.

With uncertainty, Tony makes his move. He charges at me one more time ready to strike. He comes within one step. My body comes alive. Moving as fast as a bullet, I swipe his attack with my left hand and charge my right toward his face. Tony's eyes are wide open. I see the fear. He's looking at a train he cannot avoid. One tremendous rage filled punch. A sickening crunch. Tony flies through the air landing on his back. My vision continues to tunnel, looking at Tony's motionless body without the slightest bit of sympathy.

Pure silence.

Someone clears their throat that finally penetrates the

shock. It's one of Tony's friends. They enter the Ring to help him.

My eyes fill red. One punch is not enough to satiate my thirst.

I charge toward Tony's friends. My first victim is inspecting Tony's head. He receives the blunt force of my foot that sends him into a backflip. The other two look like they're about to wet themselves. In a pitiful effort, they stand to counter my onslaught. It's futile. Within the blink of an eye, one of them is keeled over gasping for breath, while the other one is flipped over the ropes of the Ring.

Pure silence, eyes staring.

The redness doesn't quell. I'm about to hop the ropes to find my next victim when a hand pulls on my shoulder. It's Vincent, his look grave.

"We're doing this?" I ask as a question meant more as a statement.

Vincent sets in a defensive stance. "Please don't do this. You and I need to talk."

"No!" My voice bounces off the walls of the enormous room.

I charge. I feel quick and strong. I unleash a flurry of attacks. Each attack feels quicker than the last, but I don't land a single blow. Vincent is fluid in his movements. I shouldn't be surprised. He taught me everything I know about combat. My brain's erased all logic. My ability to think and focus are what makes me deadly when fighting. Right now, I'm an undisciplined crazy person against a master. This will not bode well.

As I realize how much I'm not winning, Vincent makes his first attack and connects with a right hook. I stagger to my knees with a pain screaming from the left side of my face. I spring up and throw a three-punch combination finished with a roundhouse kick. Each punch connects with air and my kick blocked. Before I can react, Vincent's foot connects with my stomach, and I fall again. My stomach feels like it could burst.

"You need to stop," Vincent demands. "My next attacks won't be so light."

He was holding back? Tears well up in my eyes, partially from the pain, but also from the helpless feeling of defeat. I give up. At least for now.

I turn my back on Vincent and leave the Ring without being dismissed.

- Chapter 34 -

Daily grind. Going through the motions. That's all I do. Attempting to flush the emotions out of my system, cleanse my body from the pain and hurt. No matter how hard I try to forget my Acropolis experience and live my old life, my memories with Lacey continue to dig in the back of my mind. I want time to fade her away. It doesn't work fast enough. Two days have passed since the incident in the Ring. I didn't suffer consequences for my actions.

When I'm not at school, I create an alternate reality for myself. I consume my spare moments with drawing and reading books. These are the only two things to help me escape.

At home, everything is back to 'normal' with a strange disconnect. My mind consumed by daydreamer thoughts, and my mother acts the same as me. I don't speak with anyone except her.

While reading a book, I hear my mother coughing in the bathroom. It's short, but it puts my senses on high alert. I rush to her.

"Everything alright?" I gasp.

My mother opens the door. "No big deal. I swallowed some air wrong." She smiles at her joke. Despite her humor, she's hiding it from me. I'm not ready to deal with this again.

After the coughing incident, I try my luck at the dispensary. I'm unable to sell my drawings, nor do I have the funds to pay for the medications, but I try to convince myself it's worth a shot. Deep down I know the reason I want to visit. Lacey. Hearing her voice may send hope.

The dispensary emerges still in rough shape from my assault. I approach it as if it is foreign, like something scary might jump out. Fear stretches out and grabs my breath. With my ID number punched, the process begins. I swear, the initialization is deliberately slow.

"How may I assist you?" comes the voice.

What was I thinking? Why did I need to fill myself with an empty bowl of hope? Of course, Lacey is not there. I punch the sign off button and leave.

This is the message telling me to settle back into my old life. Back at the Hub, I go through the motions for school activities. Hand-to-hand combat is cancelled with my group because of my rampage. Tony is nowhere to be seen since that day, but I hear he's recovering.

With everything appearing back to normal, lectures, target practice, and other endurance activities, I continue to keep my interactions with anyone, superior or equal, to a minimum. Laying low is a priority. No one seems to care much about me or take notice. Even though everything appears smooth, I wait for a ripple of waves to come charging in my direction. Something that will disrupt the peace I attempt to grant myself. Peace I want to keep.

I could see it coming from a mile away. The cue triggering the disruption of my solitude. During target practice, Vincent and Tank converse in the corner. A look shifts my way, and side by side, they strut in my direction.

Ignoring their advance, I pull the trigger of my handgun and fluidly move from target to target. A bullet hole fills the center of each one. Click. The magazine is empty. Disengaging it, a new one takes its place, avoiding eye contact with two people whom I don't want to speak.

I keep firing. Out of the corner of my eye, Vincent and Tank close the gap. A warning reaches my brain. Keeping my focus, I fire again.

The last two bullets connect with the target, another empty magazine. This is when Tank and Vincent are within breathing distance. I acknowledge their presence.

Vincent runs his hands through his hair and adjusts his glasses. Tank cracks his knuckles. I look at them with little interest.

Vincent speaks. "Your presence is requested per Quentin." His voice stays calm but firm.

Tank carries a stupid grin on his face. He laughs under a face full of hair. "How ya feelin?"

I ignore him, reload my handgun, and fasten it around my waist. "Lead on." Vincent looks relieved.

The three of us exit the shooting range. Every set of eyes turns in our direction. I can feel their stares, their questions, questions I do not have answers to.

Inside the Hub, they direct me toward the dreaded hallway. Every muscle in my body tenses. I can only imagine the terrible act Quentin wants me to perform this time.

Tank opens the door to a conference room. He makes a mock bow and delicately stretches his arm toward the inside of the room as though I am royalty. As I walk by, I want to hit him, but Tank is one of the people I don't feel confident in taking down, especially after my failed attacks on Vincent.

I enter and the scene is familiar. This is the room with the circular table and a large screen at the far end. There are a couple of other computers and a large microphone. With his back to us, Quentin sits in a chair centered in front of the large screen. In the lower right-hand corner of the screen is a digital black square.

Quentin swivels around with a look of joy. "Ah, just in time," he says with a hint of excitement. "Come on over.

Take a seat." His hand gestures an inviting wave to sit near him.

Tank makes his way to a seat. Vincent stays at the door. He gestures for me to follow Tank.

"It's D-Day men," says Quentin as he clasps his hands together, rubbing them back and forth.

Since I'm not receiving clarification on what is happening, I ask, "D-Day?"

"How rude of me," says Quentin. "I guess this is your first time. How about you explain the process to him." Quentin nods to Tank.

Tank explains, "D-Day is Draft Day. It's when we gets newbs. Ever newbs git brung here." He pauses and his short, black beard to gather his thoughts. "Theys come in with theys number and M or F on theys chest." He points at the screen and bellows out in laughter.

Vincent shoots Tank a look of annoyance and uses a thumb and a finger to rub both of his eyes underneath his glasses.

Tank throws his hands up in the air. "Wha'? It's funny. You dun wants a women when it's a man." He laughs again.

Vincent dismisses Tank and continues the explanation of the Draft. "Quentin and Valentine draft new prisoners based on their pre-established draft order."

I nod. "I'm here, why?"

Quentin turns toward me. "Well despite your little mishap, I have faith you understand your loyalties. You're no doubt a valuable asset to my organization. You have the potential to become one of these two." He points toward Vincent and Tank. "I'm going to consider you one of us, for now. I admire your guts. That makes you stand out, and I understand what that can bring for me, us. I see you sitting in this spot someday."

I swallow down the saliva built up in my mouth. His words terrify me. He's sharing the future he sees through his eyes. A future that's a possibility. Is this really all I have? The future isn't talked about much, mostly because we worry about surviving day to day. Now Quentin spells out this path, this destiny becomes real, and it's depressing. Death is always a lingering threat in the Ashen Yard. This is the first time in my life I feel death is a more suitable outcome.

Quentin sees me deep in thought. "You're always a question mark. So unpredictable, so hard to read. Who knows what's happening in there. There's no doubt you understand the severities of insubordination. You experienced that firsthand."

I nod. He's right. He doesn't know what's going through my mind. I force myself to stop thinking and be present. Living in the moment is my eighteen-year survival technique.

A static voice breaks through on the computer screen. "Preparations are nearly complete."

Vincent startles. "That's my cue." He opens the door to exit the conference room.

Tank laughs in disgust. "He cants handle it. Whatta bitch."

Vincent sharply turns and his eyes throw daggers at Tank. "You keep talking like that, and I'll make you eat those words."

Tank stops. I get the feeling Tank is a bit afraid of him. Vincent exits the room.

Once he's gone, I ask, "Why did he leave?"

Quentin turns toward the computer screen and responds, his voice muffled with his back turned against me, "He has his reasons."

Information boxes generate on the screen. Quentin filters through the information.

I look over at Tank and raise an eyebrow.

He explains, "These is specs. Info on the newbs. Like scoutin reports fer sports."

I nod and try to look at the screen, but Quentin filters through the information so fast I cannot make sense of it.

Minutes go by while Quentin reads. A voice crackles through the speakers, "Are you ready?"

Quentin pushes a button on his microphone and gives an affirmative.

The static voice replies, "We're waiting on Valentine."

"Hmph, figures," Quentin says to no one in particular. "Always waiting on that son of a bitch."

After another minute, Valentine is ready, and the go ahead is given. On Quentin's large computer screen in the small black box in the corner a face forms. It looks like it is a live feed.

"Is that Valentine?" I ask. I've never seen him before.

"Yessir," Tank replies.

I look at the face, but it's not a face. Valentine has long hair and wears a mask that covers every inch of his face, except for a hole in the mouth. The mask splits into two sides. Half of the face smiles, the other half looks sad, and there's a tear under that eye. It makes me think of split personalities.

Movement happens on the screen that pulls my attention from the mask. The new prisoners file into the center of the room displaying their numbers.

The voice crackles again as the prisoners make their way into the large room. "There are ten new prisoners in all."

Quentin sighs. "We've had worse numbers." His eyes stay glued to the screen, gathering in every physical detail on the new potential gang members. He looks at them like he's picking out the most appetizing piece of meat to put on his plate.

The first prisoner is a brute of a man. He probably stands close to six and a half feet tall. Most people at that height are as skinny as a stick. Instead, he looks like a man that would find a wall blocking his path a minor annoyance. His arms look like an art gallery. He could be Tank's twin.

Of course, this creates a buzz of excitement. Quentin

points at the screen and talks about the brute like a prize. The excitement subsides when Tank reminds Quentin that Valentine has first pick.

Quentin smashes his hands down on the sides of his chair. "Dammit Tank, why do you have to be a buzz kill?"

In the center of the room on screen, the prisoners continue filing in one by one. I count the number of prisoners on the screen. Seven so far. After the first prisoner, none of the others create much of a buzz. The eighth prisoner walks in and files in line. It's a younger, thin male. He looks no older than twelve years old. His eyes are fear ridden. I feel sorry for the kid because I doubt he'll last an hour in the Ashen Yard.

The first female comes into view. My vision becomes paralyzed. It's the perfect blend of brown and blonde hair with those stunning green eyes I'll never forget.

- Chapter 35 -

Why is Lacey here? The voices of Quentin and Tank bounce through the air. My ears are deaf to their words. As I look at the large screen, time stands still. This must be an out of body experience like living someone else's life. My stature is threatened, and I place my hand on the table to keep my balance from a sudden surge of dizziness.

An impending war slowly pursues us, but my war just began. Fear and excitement battle within my core. Seeing Lacey, the blood rushes to my heart and fills me with hope. Someone I never thought I would see again stands within my vision. The fear kicks in. Why is she here? The Ashen Yard is not safe for anyone, especially a new girl like her.

Lacey stands in line like the rest of the new prisoners. Her appearance isn't elaborate like I'm used to seeing. Her clothes are ragged and filled with dirt. Her hair bends in different directions like she was just dragged out of bed from a dead sleep. Her hands hang down with her fingers interlaced. The nerves make her thumbs fidget.

Quentin's whiny voice is what regains my conscious to the world. He's clearly upset. "This Draft doesn't really matter," he says. "Valentine is going to pick that big guy and there isn't much except the bottom of the barrel after that. Besides..," he glances behind his shoulder and remembers he's not alone.

"Never mind."

I wonder if Quentin and Valentine work together? My instincts say yes.

"The Draft is just picking prisoners to be new gang members?" I ask.

Tank nods. "Yes." Tank pounds his fists on the counter. "Quentin's right. This wastin' our damn time!"

Quentin chimes in. "Think of it like sports. The team that struggles gets more benefits from the draft to strengthen their team. That's the mutual agreement."

"How fitting," I reply. "Because this is all a game."

Quentin gives me a look of warning. "Control that spunk. Don't take it lightly that I admire you." An odd fit of laughter comes and Quentin relaxes in his chair. "This is the system you've been living all your life. Order requires structure. You benefit from our structure." He raises his eyebrows like he made the determining argument of a case and returns his attention to the screen.

He cannot be serious. I wouldn't wish my life upon anyone no matter what. Quentin's logic sickens me. Playing a puppet of death for warlords within a twisted systemic structure is the culmination of hell.

I mutter under my breath. "This is stupid." I think my comment is low enough that it doesn't reach Quentin's ears, but he swivels toward me in his chair, and I know I'm mistaken.

He moves with his uncharacteristic speed and whips the cane toward my face. My reflexes catch it in my hand.

Still looking at the cane, I rotate my head to look at him. "That won't be necessary."

At first, his face gets that crazy, twisted look. The switch flips and he's amused. Maniacally laughing, again. "I'm glad you're on my side. You're good." He slides his chair a couple of inches next to me, hobbles up to his feet, and puts his arm around my neck. "You've done good things for me my boy. I look forward to further results."

The static filled voice interrupts our moment. "All prisoners are on display. You know the procedure. State the number of the prisoner you wish to acquire."

Quentin presses his microphone button, "Looks like Valentine's up," he says.

To no one's surprise, Valentine chooses the monstrous prisoner. "Valentine's pick is #25294M." It's funny to hear him speak in the third person, but it makes sense for the speaker on the other side of the radio to distinguish who's talking.

The static voice speaks after the selection. "Prisoner #25294M please step forward." The brute complies and steps forward with a swagger. "Please proceed to your left through the door."

The man disappears from our sight.

"That son of a," mutters Quentin. He points at me. "I designate you to take care of him. I know you can do it."

This must be another one of Quentin's initiations to prove my worth.

Quentin looks at Tank. "Who're you thinking?"

Tank plays with his beard. "Third from left."

"Same," Quentin replies and turns toward me. "You thinking the same?"

I gulp. No, that's not what I'm thinking. I hesitate. Screw it. I have nothing to lose. "What about the girl?"

The two of them stare at me blankly. Then they look at each other and burst into laughter. Quentin laughs so hard he wipes tears from his eyes. "You're killing me."

My cheeks flush. It was worth a shot.

"So yeah, I'm going with the guy." Quentin pushes the button on his microphone and speaks. "Quentin selects #29297M." Like the first prisoner, this one gets directions and heads off screen.

Looking at the rest of the prisoners, it's hard to rationalize why Quentin would pick Lacey. She's the daintiest prisoner, apart from the young boy who looks like he hasn't reached puberty.

Shortly after Quentin's pick, Valentine selects another one of the male prisoners.

The back-and-forth selection of prisoners progresses until there're three prisoners to select from: Lacey, the young boy, and another. If Lacey has a chance to join Quentin's side, this is the time we pick her because I have a feeling Valentine will choose her over the young one.

Quentin converses with Tank when I cut in. "We should take the girl," I interject.

A slim smile moves its way upon Quentin's face. "You dirty dog. Do you fancy this girl? You have a little crush? Let's see if the stars are meant to align." Quentin sounds like a parent attempting to embarrass their child.

Tank whistles. "She sure cute."

Quentin mocks him. "Oh, come on Tank. Not you too. Don't be such a dirty old man."

Silence staggers the room for a few seconds.

Quentin grabs hold of the microphone. Before he speaks, his head dramatically turns facing me. It's like he's challenging me. His mouth rattles off a prisoner number that does not belong to Lacey.

The prisoner steps and disappears. The next few moments feel cruel and unwanted. Lacey and the young boy stand there fidgeting. Valentine speaks, "Valentine's last pick is #25302F."

Lacey's eyes stream with tears before her head drops and her hair covers her face. She moves to her left with shoulders sunk in defeat. Before she leaves our sight, she looks up at the screen. My heart stops. It feels like her eyes plead for my help. She's gone.

I try to process my feelings, but they're interrupted when the last prisoner, the young boy, completely breaks down. Looking like a toddler too tired, he falls to the ground sobbing a river and curls up in the fetal position. Two guards have a difficult time grabbing him because he thrashes about like a wild animal. One of them grabs his club and swings it for his head. The session terminates before the act is complete, and we sit with a blank screen in front of us.

Quentin and Tank poke fun at the boy's tantrum. My brain rattles a plan. Even though Lacey is not coming to Quentin's territory, she's still nearby. My decision is final. I will do whatever it takes to find her.

"Thank you for preventing this from being the least dramatic Draft we have had in a while," Quentin says and spits on the ground. "And most pathetic. If it wasn't for you and your girlfriend, this would've been a snooze fest." Quentin and Tank give me stupid grins.

When I don't play into their game, Quentin directs toward Tank, "You know what to do. Go greet our new members and break them in."

"Yes, sir," barks Tank. His massive form lifts from his chair, which groans as if it is regaining its breath. Tank salutes and exits the conference room.

"Why're you standing there?" Quentin whines. "Make yourself useful and get out of here."

I gratefully take my leave. I need to think and develop a plan. While walking down the giant staircase in the foyer to leave the Hub, Vincent stands at the bottom. I'm not sure how to interpret his absence during the Draft.

Vincent's eyes are tired. Deep lines litter his face. He looks like he's fighting an unwanted battle.

I reach the bottom of the steps. I nod at Vincent and try to walk past him. He reaches out and grabs my arm. His voice is barely above a whisper, "Don't do anything stupid."

"What the hell is that supposed to mean?" I spit.

"I have a feeling you're going to act rash."

I twist out of his grip and exit the Hub.

- Chapter 36 -

The speed of my sprint is nothing compared to the speed of my thoughts. The Draft changes everything. Whatever actions I take, they'll have to be rogue. There's no one I can rely on. The only person I trust is my mother, and she's in no shape to help. I used to trust Vincent, but it wavers on a thread. It's me against the world. What happens if I do find Lacey? She's owned by Valentine. I'll figure something out.

Sprinting up the stairs to my apartment, I race into the kitchen where my mother cooks pasta on the stove. She turns with a smile that instantly melts to concern.

"Is everything alright?" she asks.

Even though I'm in shape, I rest my hands upon my knees to catch my breath. "It's complicated," I reply with a strained voice. I take a seat to aid my recovery.

Worry draws upon her face. "What's wrong?"

"You know the girl I met in the Acropolis, Lacey?" I ask.

She gives a nod.

"I saw her today."

"Oh really? How?" Before I answer, she turns and tends to the pasta.

"She's a prisoner now."

My mother's hands stop stone cold. Her jaw drops. "You can't be serious."

"I was apparently accepted into Quentin's inner circle. Hooray for me." I reinforce my sarcasm with the wave of my hands like I'm celebrating. "I saw my first Draft. I watched as new prisoners entered the screen. Lacey was one of them."

My mother asks a question she already knows the answer to, "Who got her?"

"Valentine."

"Are you going to try and find her?" she asks.

I rub my eyes. "That's the plan."

"What's holding you back?" She stirs again.

"It's Vincent. He told me not to act rash because he knows I will. You know, I always looked up to him until a few days ago. I felt like he was watching out for me. There're things he's not telling me, and I don't appreciate being left in the dark."

My mother stops and thinks for a moment. "I've always liked Vincent."

I hold my hands up. "Wait, hold on. You're telling me you like the same guy that sliced your arm while you were bound and gagged? Really?"

She shrugs. "I don't know. I've always felt he's bound by his situation. Maybe he'd be different if Quentin wasn't in charge."

"Maybe you're right," I mutter. "But I still don't trust him."

"He's the one who told me your father died on that dreadful night."

"Wait, he told you?" This strikes my chest like one of Vincent's punches.

She nods. "I could tell he was truly sorry. I could read the sadness and anger in his eyes."

"You're just telling me this now? What's the point of that?"

"I think dinner is ready. Are you hungry?"

I hold up my hand. "You're not getting a pass on this. Tell me what you know."

Her eyes are exhausted. "The truth. The truth is I don't have much to tell you. He showed up and delivered the news. I was already sick from being pregnant. It hurt." She rubs her eyes. "He hugged me and walked off. I knew he was watching you. He'd hang back in the distance. At first, I thought he was looking after me, which maybe he was. But when you started going to school and you would always come home and tell me what he taught you, I knew he was looking out for you."

My mind wanders. I think back to my early days of school. Many times he'd give me an extra session or pull me aside to share his sage advice. "How well did he know my father?"

She shrugs. "I mean, they worked together with Quentin, but other than that, I don't know."

The water boils over and requires my mother's attention. She tends to the noodles and finishes preparing the meal.

I want to talk to Vincent, but I don't have the time and my stomach yells for food.

We both fix our plates and sit down at the table. My mother asks, "What's your plan?"

"I have no idea. I'm going to grab my gear and figure something out on the way."

"That sounds dangerous."

"The story of my life."

My mother coughs into her napkin. It's more intense. She pulls the napkin away from her mouth and quickly sets it down.

"Let me see the napkin," I demand. She hesitates, and then presents it. There are small specks of red splattered across the white. My shoulders sink. "It's coming back."

Wetness mists my mother's eyes. "I'm afraid so," her voice quivers.

Instead of being defeated, I look at her with confidence. "I'll make some change. Look at us. Look at our life. This is going nowhere. We dance with death every day. I don't know what I'm going to do, but something will change."

I reach out to take my mother's hand. "I haven't let you down yet, and I don't plan on starting now."

With tear-soaked eyes, my mother musters a meager smile. "I know."

I scarf down my dinner and head to my bedroom to gather my necessities. I open my closet door and unlock my chest. Inside is where I keep my extra gear in case of emergencies. I'm armed with two handguns, twelve magazines, a combat knife, a flashlight, and my lighter. My last necessity is a tiny backpack I fill with water and snacks.

I'm about to say farewell to my mother, but she stops me. "It's going to be dark in a couple of hours. Why don't you at least wait until then?"

Her logic is sound. Working at night is more ideal. I recognize how little of a plan I've formulated, and I should be more thoughtful.

I reside in the fact that I need to wait. Back inside my room, I pull out the crate of books. Since I finished the science fiction book about the pilot, I rustle through the different titles to select something new. Most of the books I have read at least once. Spotting a title I haven't read, I grab it, turn it over, and read the synopsis. The book is about a young boy and girl who fall in love. According to an unspoken rule, they're not supposed to see each other. This book seems fitting to my life. An author's quote at the bottom raves it is a modern-day Romeo and Juliet.

I nestle into bed, cozy up, and read. Within the first couple of chapters, I cannot help but laugh because of how my life correlates with the story. I read until the light becomes too dim.

Heading into the kitchen, my mother sits at the table staring into space.

"It's time," I say.

She snaps out of her stupor and stands up. She embraces me, "I love you," she whispers.

"I love you too." I reassure her I'll be back. With the night's final goodbyes, I take my leave.

As I bound down the stairs, I look toward the west. Even though I've never been to Valentine's headquarters, I know its general direction.

As I jog, the streets stand eerily quiet, even for this time of night. Normally a few stragglers wander around. Not that I am complaining, but it fills me with uneasiness.

My mind prepares a plan. When I reach Valentine's territory, my hope is that the setup is nearly identical to Quentin's. Heading to the residential district is my best shot. This makes sense for two reasons: First, it will probably be quiet like it is here, and second, I'll be able to take someone by surprise and force information out of them. If I have no luck, I guess I'll try and infiltrate Valentine's Hub, however that will work.

As I run, I look to my right and see Quentin's Hub. Just like the residential district, it's quiet, almost peaceful. I hope this calm lasts.

Still quiet, still nothing. I'm in the thick woods that act as the great divide between the east and west. I feel safer within the confines of the cluster of trees.

The quiet is interrupted by an explosion large enough to send a vibration that reverberates under my feet. I startle and freeze. It happened behind me. I turn and calculate the position. It's near Quentin's Hub.

So, Valentine strikes first.

Warning sirens fill my ears, the siren for battle. I know Quentin hinted at war, but I didn't think it'd happen so quickly.

"Dammit," I mutter. I'm conflicted. This means there will be less security at Valentine's and easier to infiltrate. If I don't report for duty, I will be a marked as a target to both sides of the conflict. Reporting for duty will make it appear I'm participating in the war instead of looking for Lacey. The decision becomes easy, and I turn around.

- Chapter 37 -

Sprinting back toward Quentin's Hub, my senses stay on high alert. At any moment, I could run into Valentine's men. No more explosions happen after the initial blast, which is odd.

I don't encounter any enemies on my journey back. As I approach the large steps, an army of Quentin's men gather around. Quentin, Tank, and Vincent stand at the top of the stairs.

This is it. This is the war. Quentin will not back down. He looks pissed. He's barking orders.

My thoughts turn to Lacey. She'll be on the opposite side of this war. I wonder how I'm going to locate her.

The damage to the Hub is minimal. I see the mangled body of a victim from the bombing. If my eyes don't deceive me, it's the young kid drafted last who had the meltdown. From the looks of it, he died instantly. It was probably for the best. He didn't stand a chance in here.

Numbers of gang members filter in around the large stairway to the Hub. They congregate in their pre-designated groups.

While I watch, Vincent waves at me to come to the top of the stairway. Bounding three steps at a time like a hurdler, I join the ranks of Quentin, Vincent, and Tank.

Shortly after, Tony joins us. He gives me a quick, unsure look. This is not the time to address the petty problems between us. I pat him on the shoulder. "This is war, and we have our duties." He nods.

Quentin cusses up a storm. Saliva flies out of his mouth as he yells. All members look fearful of him but direct their attention toward Vincent and Tank. Quentin's slew of curses doesn't give the leadership his minions need.

Vincent's concentration focuses on Tony and me. "As you can see, Quentin's upset." He pulls out radios and headsets. "Both of you will get commander headsets. These will allow access to the commander channel. Quentin can override any communication and give direct orders to any of us. Be alert at all times." He tosses the radios and headsets.

I clip the small radio to the inside of my coat jacket. Placing the speaker into my ear, I execute a sound check. Vincent gives me the thumbs up.

"Heys you! Gets over here," Tank barks to Tony.

Tony moves as quickly as possible. Tank smacks him on the back of the head once he reaches him and asks what took him so long.

Feeling a bit relieved I'm staying with Vincent, I double check my gear. Vincent rests his hand on my shoulder. Pulling my attention toward him, I wait for his directive.

"Quentin feels it is best you engage solo." His voice serious.

I salute, but a troubling thought occurs. "But what is my objective?" I ask.

He brushes his hand over his mouth before speaking again. "Your objective is to infiltrate Valentine's headquarters and in Quentin's words, 'cause some mayhem.'"

It feels like a giant red target is painted on my torso. Not that I should care because I have my own secret objective, but it still infuriates me Quentin would send me in for such a dangerous job. "So, what you're saying is Quentin wants me dead?"

Vincent tries to speak, but I deny him the chance. "Aside from this place, Valentine's headquarters is the most heavily guarded building in the Ashen Yard. And I'm supposed to walk in and," I put my hands up with finger quotes, "cause some mayhem? What the hell does that even mean?" I glance over at Quentin. He's still being a filthy mouthed old man.

Vincent ignores my fit. With a reassuring tone, he speaks, "Look, I'm confident you'll be fine."

I should shoot Quentin right here and now. What a selfish, no-good bastard. In this moment, I make the decision I will take Quentin down. Now is not the time though. Lacey is my number one priority.

"Let me explain the strategy," Vincent says. "Tank, Tony, and I command everyone. My squad is defending our Hub. Tank's squad is headed to their Warehouse District. Tony's squad to their Residential District." He makes sure I'm paying attention to his details.

I gaze at him with determined eyes. Satisfied, he continues, "Quentin wants you to sneak your way through the heart of the battle between Tank and Tony's squad. He feels the squads will create distractions and cover your advance." He pauses and looks over his shoulder before continuing. "However, I'm going to advise you to flank around the outside of the Residential District. My battle intuition says this is the best strategy."

I heavy sigh. "Whatever."

"Don't make your move until our squads have assembled. They have to engage before you make your move."

"There's one thing I've noticed," I say. "I don't see any of Valentine's members."

Vincent's brow furrows. "I noticed that too. Quentin's convinced it is him. But you're right, there's no sign of further conflict."

"You think this has to do with that military looking group I saw before?"

Vincent adjusts his glasses and places his hand on his chin. "Either way, Quentin's ready to do this. He wants to shake things up."

"You guys are idiots. You realize that don't you?" I stare hard at Vincent. Even if Vincent is bound by Quentin, the guy has a brain for himself, and he doesn't seem to use it. This only reaffirms the fact I cannot rely on anybody.

Vincent looks indifferent. The fact I insulted him doesn't faze him. Instead, he puts both hands on my shoulders and squeezes. He looks over his shoulder at Quentin and pulls me to the side. "I know you want to find the girl. I know for a fact she's in Valentine's headquarters."

I look at him in bewilderment. "How do you know about her?"

Vincent looks annoyed. "Trust me. I know she's there. The next time we see each other, I need to tell you some things. Clear up my conscience."

I have no idea what he means, nor do I care. Do I trust the man my mother trusts? I never know which Vincent I'm talking to. There were many times he treated me like a father treats his son. The betrayal I feel towards him lingers. I take his words with a grain of salt.

I turn and walk away from Vincent. I sit down near the front door of the Hub and wait.

With the final preparations complete, the squads march off in their respective directions.

Vincent approaches. "You are clear to engage in your assignment."

I nod and do one final gear check. Satisfied, I descend down the Hub's steps and jog toward the southwest.

Only a few minutes into my journey and a buzz fills my ears. It's Vincent. "One more thing. Keep an open mind."

This mysterious puzzle talk pisses me off. "Obviously,

there's something you need to say." No response. Vincent deliberately ignored my statement, or he's busy giving orders to his squad. I think it's the former.

Frustrated by odd comments and unanswered questions, I maintain my pace and trek along my designated path.

My hope is I can quickly find Lacey. Sometimes women who fight cut their hair off, so their gender is not a dead giveaway. Women are considered weak targets. Other times they bun their hair and hide it under head protection. I need to be aware.

The commotion and daydreaming keeps me from realizing how crisp the air is. The subtle bite of cold is like a dagger of freshness. My breath releases small white clouds.

I run inside the thick forest divide, where I turned around earlier in the evening. Another couple hundred feet and I'll proceed into the thicker part of the forest. The trees feel like a protective barrier.

Explosions and gunshots strike from the northwest. The signal of war. I slide up against a tree and listen. Faded shouts fly through the air. I wonder how many of us will die today.

I peak my head around the tree in the direction of the fighting. A bright flash pierces through the darkness creating a flare.

Despite the sounds of war, I hear a muffled, crunching sound of dry foliage. It sounds like a foot snapped a twig. Both handguns are ready to fire. I slide down the trunk of the tree and crouch. Focusing my mind, I ignore the sounds of battle and listen carefully. Nothing. I don't dare move an inch, hoping my ears pick up sounds from my not-so-distant enemy.

Another crunch comes from my right. Aiming my handguns in the direction, I creep along the ground in a squat scanning for movement. Nobody's there, not even a shadow. Time slows to a lull.

A figure emerges from behind a tree. For a brief second,

we see each other, and our eyes open wide. We both fire awkward shots and miss before we conceal behind the trees.

I curse myself. If the circumstances were normal, he'd be done for. But the circumstances are not normal. I hesitated. I had to make sure it wasn't Lacey.

Shots pummel my tiny bit of protection, and they come from multiple directions. Great, there's more than one.

Rolling from my tree, I aim in my initial target's direction. My target peaks around his tree exposing part of his torso. I fire off two shots. Both connect with his body, one in the shoulder and the other in his neck. He falls lifeless.

More bullets fly in my direction about twenty yards parallel from my first victim. I slide back into protection.

Calculating the location in my head, I steady myself for a quick attack. With my left hand, I point my gun around the tree with half my head exposed. I fire a burst of three shots. Returning fire welcomes my attack from the next tree over. Thanks for the information.

I bend down and grab a rock. I toss it to the side hitting the tree next to me. Shots fire toward the tree. I step out from my protection fully exposing my body with both guns aimed. My target's head is covered in a battle helmet. I don't have time to second guess. My instincts fire. My target jerks with each bullet that connects. The body falls against the ground hard. The impact makes the combat helmet roll off.

I stand paralyzed. Flowing out from underneath the helmet is a mop of light brown hair. My gut turns. I think I just killed Lacey.

- Chapter 38 -

Nightmares haunt my senses. How long have I been standing here? Why did she wear a helmet? Why did she hide her face from me?

I snap out of it. Maybe she's still alive. "Lacey!" I yell.

Sprinting toward her body, my pace is abruptly interrupted. An explosion expands through the surroundings. My body lifts from the ground like a leaf blowing in the wind. Colliding with a tree, I freefall toward the ground landing with an impact cushioned by shrubbery. The air is siphoned from my lungs. Each attempt at a breath stabs my chest like a knife. A fiery acidic burn slathers my throat. A sharp ringing bombards my hearing like a loud warning siren.

Water wells up in my eyes and tears streams down. Even through the blurry mirror of tears, I observe plumes of smoke intoxicating the air.

Wiping my eyes a few times, I conjure up a semi coherent picture of the scene. It doesn't look pretty. I'm vulnerable, and I don't like it.

Covering my mouth, I gather my composure at the pace of an old man. I attempt to stand up and get out of this mess. My disorientation questions my bearings and balance. My mind clears, and I remember Lacey.

My legs stagger in the direction where I think the explosion happened. I walk about fifteen feet when I realize I don't know how far I was thrown. The combination of smoke and dizziness isn't helping. My eyes move toward the ground trying to find evidence of my recent gunfight.

I shake my head as though it will help the ringing. I realize my headset is gone. My communication is severed. I feel my waist to see if I have my guns. There's nothing. I did not holster them before the explosions. They could be anywhere. Now panic really settles in. In a war like this, my handguns are my lifeline.

I drop down to my hands and knees to lay low and scour the ground for anything useful. My hand runs into something metallic. I feel the familiar handle of one my handguns and breathe a sigh of relief. The other one should be close by. My sense of security rises.

I raise my gun to the faded shadows. The heat from the explosion becomes more intense as I continue to move. A bright light dances in the distance.

My eyes spot an empty shell case on the ground. Closing my eyes, I imagine my position prior to shooting those fatal rounds. Guess work is no longer needed when the shadows of two bodies stand over Lacey. They both wear the gray uniforms. The same ones I saw during my solo mission.

One of them scans her face. A green light illuminates through the haze. He sighs, "Looks like we killed one."

The other one shrugs. "Collateral damage. We can't save them all."

Save who?

They drag the body away and pass the other man I shot and killed. They're ignoring him.

Without thinking, I yell, "Hey," with my handgun at the ready.

They drop the body and swing their rifles from their shoulders. I fire shots in their direction. One of them falls to the ground. The other fires at me. I tuck and roll out of the way, taking sanctuary behind another tree.

"You're making a mistake," the man shouts. "I don't want to harm you."

I yell back, "What a load of crap."

I hear a gunshot. I expect it to come in my direction, but instead hear yelps of pain coming from the men.

I peak around the corner and see one lying motionless, while the other lies on the ground clutching his chest. More gunshots fire, but this time in my direction. The shots come from a blue shirt, Valentine's.

This person is not well trained. He keeps his body out in the open and stands firing. I round the corner, fire at him, and connect as though he were a stationary target at the shooting range.

With Valentine's agent no longer a threat, I walk over to the person in the gray uniform. He clutches his chest, a wound near his heart pours blood painting his chest red.

He looks up with painful eyes. Blood lines his mouth.

I disregard his pain. My angry hands clench his gray uniform. "What're you doing? Why are you doing this?" My screams pierce the air.

He attempts to speak, but pain and blood make him gargle. Before his eyes roll up into his head, he mutters one word, "Prisonborn."

"What about Prisonborns!" My scream receives no answer. Is he part of the reason why Prisonborns are missing? What do these guys want with us?

I shudder out of my confusion and look around. There's no sign of Lacey. I move toward where I last remember seeing her, but more gunshots fire in my direction. One shot grazes my left arm and a thin red line traces the skin. I raise my gun and fire one shot in the perceived direction. My enemies hide in the background. More shots scream my way, and I roll on the ground in retreat. Whoever is shooting is more experienced in their tactics. Another tree turns into my protection. It looks like my time runs out and I run.

More gunshots reverberate from the northwest. The groups are engaged, and I need to get to my position. Maybe Vincent speaks the truth. Maybe it wasn't Lacey I shot. Maybe she really is inside Valentine's headquarters. He told me with certainty that she's there. Despite my faltering trust in his words, they are what I have to hold onto.

Despite my battle bruises and bleeding arm, I'm reinvigorated with hope and relief. My stated objective now dominates my thoughts.

I move through the forest a couple hundred more feet. I'm greeted by an area with blood stains but no bodies. I wonder if more people in gray uniforms are around.

A few more minutes continuing forward, and I'm close to penetrating the other side of the great forest divide. That'll mean I'll officially be in Valentine's territory. My target is near, and hopefully my objective will be complete.

Another explosion blasts again, and for the second time in less than an hour, I spiral backwards. Feeling my body fly through the air is soothing and terrifying all at once. I collide with a hard surface. Everything goes black.

- Chapter 39 -

I stir into consciousness. I'm not sure how long I was out, but the sky is still dark, so I assume not for long. While lying on my back, I notice a sharp pain piercing the back of my head. The acrid smell of smoke lingers in the air engulfing my lungs with fire. My eyes feel like iron curtains. Instead of fighting the weight, I keep them closed. Testing my extremities, I assess there's movement in all areas of my body. My body aches like it was used as a punching bag. I muster my arms up toward my head. My hands touch a slippery liquid and slide across my hair.

I make a failed attempt to turn onto my side. It takes me three attempts to complete the action. My eyes slide open and fill with a blurry image. I blink a couple of times to gain focus. There's a small circle of scarred trees from the blast with a haze of smoke that floats like a mist.

Clouds fill my mind. Every attempt to move requires concentration and effort, which bombards my aching head. My body forces a command inside my head. Place both hands on the ground. Get on your knees. Apply pressure to your hands. My movements, although strenuous, become manageable.

I gather my bearings and complete an inventory check. My utility belt is gone. Somehow, I managed to hold on to my one handgun. I check the magazine. Only five bullets line the inside. I silently curse as I scan the vicinity. There's no sign of my utility belt, but my eyes do find a small black bag. Near the bag is the body of a younger person. No movement, not even a slight stir. He's dressed in a gray uniform. His face is young, too young. It saddens me to know that someone else out there is sacrificing the world's youth.

I limp in the boy's direction. With each step I look for movement. Nothing. I check the neck for a pulse. He's as dead as the trees around me. I look for identification on the body with no luck. I check his body for weaponry. My scrounging for weapons comes up fruitless, but I do find a bottled water, a packaged granola snack, and first aid supplies.

I become aware of the eerie quietness. Prior to my unconscious state, gunfire and explosions pulsed through the air. The sounds of battle, the voices shouting commands, the footsteps all absent. The only sound is the tiny crackle of fire licking the trees.

I dismiss my paranoia and take advantage of the first aid supplies. Bandaging up my head is my number one priority. I apply gauze to the back of it. My hands come back bloody. I apply more gauze and put pressure on the wound. My vision blurs and my hands brace to the ground.

I sit down and have my scavenged meal. My initial instinct is to drink the entire bottle of water in one gigantic chug and scarf the granola in one bite. I resist the urge and pace myself. I take one controlled sip of water and take a kid sized bite from the granola, savoring every piece of the meal. The time allows my body to reset as much as it can in its current state.

I look back at the dead boy. Was he the cause of the explosions earlier? Where did he come from? He doesn't work for Quentin, so does he work for Valentine? There's no point continuing to ask questions that will not be answered. My immediate priority is moving forward.

Positioning myself toward Valentine's territory, I set in a

slow, steady pace. The blow to my head and loss of blood makes the ground teeter in unexpected ways. Several times I stop to prevent my body from collapsing. My current meager state makes me vulnerable. My confidence falters.

The further I walk through the forest, the less the environment appears to be destroyed. Walking through the trees, I approach a clearing. Stretching into the open are a bundle of warehouses that look similar to our Warehouse District.

Several of Valentine's gang members patrol the area. The color of their blue shirts stand out from the distance. There's no sense of urgency or panic amongst the group. That only means the fighting hasn't reached them yet.

The distinct sound of footsteps captures my attention. My judgment tells me the potential threat is within thirty feet.

Crouching down, I hold my handgun. The footsteps come closer. Although the details are unclear, I make out the shape of the person and see the distinguished size. A couple more steps and I realize it's the monster of a human Valentine drafted.

My mind assesses the situation, and I determine firing shots at him will draw attention from the others around the warehouses. This would be a poor decision, especially with my limited ammo. It would stack the odds against me.

Instead, I ready to take advantage of the element of surprise. Anticipating his approach, I load my legs ready to spring. Each passing second reduces the gap. Ten feet, five feet. The timing is right. I move but something is wrong. The ground shifts, I lose balance, and stumble right into his line of sight.

Startled, the brute takes a step back. He fumbles with his weapon. Although my plan doesn't work as intended, his confusion opens the door to draw my gun. All thoughts of keeping my attack quiet fly out the window. After I take him out, I'll take his gun and deal with anyone else.

Steadying my gun, I aim and pull the trigger. A sickening "click." No bullet releases from the barrel. I keep pulling the trigger with the same result. Each time the sad sound vomits out the mouth of the gun.

An amusing smile spreads across his face. His gun is pulled, but he doesn't shoot.

"Looks like you got trouble," he says.

He slides his gun back into its holster. He's sizing me up. He sees an injured, battered up target who appears to have no means to protect himself. His assessment is correct.

He kinks his neck from left to right, each time I hear a snap, crackle, and pop. In a few moments, he'll beat me to a pulp.

Even with all my training, this massive brute would be a challenge on a good day. I fear my chances are slim in my current condition. I almost wish he'd shoot rather than pummel me.

I stand up in a fighting position. His eyes laugh. To stand a chance, I must finish this quick.

"I hope you said your prayers," he sneers.

He charges like a raging bull hell-bent on piercing the color red.

- Chapter 40 -

My assailant pummels me with his shoulder square in the chest. I fly backwards, a feeling I'm becoming used to, and land on my back with a sickening thud. My brain tells me to breathe, but my lungs argue.

I wiggle and squirm on the ground for a taste of oxygen. As I struggle, a massive shape looms over me like an eclipse.

"Having a hard time breathing?" he growls. "Let me help." Reaching down, he wraps his massive hand around my neck. His fingers almost overlap around his thumb.

Black dots sprinkle around my vision like ugly confetti. I must act before I pass out and lay at his mercy. I must complete my objective and keep the promise I gave my mother.

Instead of pinning me, he kneels on one knee. In a last-ditch effort to save my life, I swing my knee up and connect with his jewels.

His eyes open wide. The only sound that escapes his mouth is a breathy, "Uh." His grip loosens around my neck as he falls over. He struggles on the ground with both hands holding onto his manhood. Wiggling, moving, and moaning makes him look like an overgrown child.

I wish I could savor my victory, but my will to stand up cannot overcome the pain in my body. I lie on the ground inhaling deep. My head swells, my back stings, even my little toe hurts. I muster the will to stagger to my feet.

My enemy recovers and releases a deep yell of rage. "I'm going to make you hurt so bad."

This draws the attention of Valentine's other gang members. I see them rush in our direction out of the corner of my eye.

The brute charges again. I'm prepared in a battle stance and calculate his footsteps. As soon as his right foot lands, I jump with my legs tucked and extend a flying kick that connects above his knee cap. My foot lands with a sickening crack. His body moves forward but his leg bends backwards.

His screams pierce the air. I run over to my victim and punch him in the face. He brings his hands up for protection. I move in and grab his gun from his waist. That's when I feel the barrel of a gun press up against the back of my head.

"I wouldn't do that if I were you," says a voice behind me.

I raise my hands in the air. There's no point in fighting. Whoever's behind me doesn't shoot. Maybe I have a chance. I face my enemy and see I'm surrounded with guns pointed.

They look at the brute I successfully dismembered. The one who seems to be the leader asks, "What the hell did you do?"

My lips stay sealed.

He approaches me and puts the gun to my forehead. "You think you're something special?" He spits on his fallen comrade. "You're pathetic."

Whimpers come from him. "It hurts." He clutches his knee and wiggles around.

"Valentine expected way more out of you," says the leader. He points his gun at him and fires. His wiggling stops.

The others laugh. It sounds nervous. The action of the leader is disgusting. It's something Quentin would do, completely inhuman. When I survive this situation, this pathetic man will become my target, and my lack of empathy toward him will make it easy.

He draws his attention to me. "Where were we?" He points his gun to my forehead again.

Before he can continue, one of the other members says, "Wait, Mike, isn't this the guy Valentine wants?"

The leader, Mike, scans me up and down, thinking. He grabs my face and turns it from side to side examining my features. "I think you're right."

Valentine wants me? I've never met the guy. What does he want with me? How does he know who I am?

"We hit the jackpot," says Mike.

Celebratory whoops and high fives are shared amongst the group. I debate whether to make a move because I could catch Mike by surprise, use him as a shield, and possibly take out the others. But the knowledge that Valentine wants me negates the thought. This could get me closer to my personal objective, Lacey, assuming it wasn't her I encountered earlier.

"Pat him down," orders Mike.

One of Mike's pawns abides his command. Even though most of my firepower is diminished, he strips me of anything they find threatening.

Something is pulled over my face. My world goes black. I think it's a shirt. It smells terrible like sweat. My hands are bound together. I'm pushed from behind. There's no point in resisting.

My captors guide me for about fifteen minutes. They push me, mock me, and make jokes amongst each other like they're good friends. At one point my head gets woozy, and I stagger to my knees. Curses come my way, and I'm forced up. Mike orders his men to assist me.

We walk up some steps, and I assume we're at Valentine's headquarters. Inside, I'm escorted up more stairs. My mind pictures the foyer inside of Quentin's Hub.

We come to another stopping point. Mike speaks, "Valentine, we have the one you're looking for." There's a buzz, and a door opens. I'm not forced to move anywhere.

"What do you think we're going to get?" asks another member.

"I hope it's some booze," says another. "I want to get faded." They laugh in agreement.

I hear the door open again and the leader comes out. "What did he say, Mike?"

Mike sounds disappointed when he speaks, "He wants him cleaned up."

"But don't we get a reward?" one whines.

Mike snaps, "I don't know. He's in no mood to talk."

They escort me again and we enter a room. I'm pushed on to a soft surface, my blindfold removed.

Mike's the only one in the room. His dark eyes filled with spite. His lip curls in a snarl. Obviously, he was prepared for more praise from Valentine.

"I should've killed you," he says.

I laugh. "You're right. You don't want to meet me on an even playing field. You wouldn't stand a chance." I muster a smug look.

He backhands me across the face. The force knocks me onto my side, fortunately on the soft surface of the bed. "You're a cocky one. I hope I get the opportunity." He spits in my face and leaves the room.

I rub my face across the blanket of the bed. The bed feels welcoming. My eyes close and I drift off.

It's difficult to tell time when you fall asleep, but I think I sleep for maybe a half an hour before the door wakes me up. A man dressed in scrubs with a stethoscope enters.

"Hi," he says. He looks nervous.

"Hi," I reply.

"I don't want any trouble. I'm ordered to aid your injuries and patch you up before you see Valentine."

I nod. He appears kind.

"I'm going to help you sit up," the doctor says. He walks

over to me, and between his help and my effort, I'm sitting upright. It hurts.

The doctor unwraps my bandage around my head. When he pulls the cloth away, it's stained dark red. He disposes it before moving behind me. His gloved hands move through my hair.

"That's a pretty nasty gash you got. It's nothing a few stitches can't fix. I'm going to apply some antiseptic swabs. It's going to sting."

He applies the swabs. I wince but overall feel more refreshed. He moves in front of me. "I'll be right back. I need to grab the stitches."

Once he leaves, my shoulders relax, and I think about Lacey. I wonder if the doctor knows anything about her.

He returns and I'm thankful it is only him because I feel like we can have a conversation.

He pulls out a syringe and a bottle. Inserting the needle into the bottle, he pulls it back, and it fills with a clear liquid. "This is the numbing serum. It's going to sting like the swab."

"No problem," I reply. "Thank you for patching me up."

"I should be thanking you for being cooperative. I mean, I've heard about you."

Caught surprised again. "Am I notorious over here?"

"Well, yes. You're sort of a legend. Valentine's been trying to get you over here for a few years now. You've evaded every attempt."

"Huh," is all I muster.

"Alright, here it comes." There's another sting, and the top of my head goes numb. I feel the pressure of his hands doing his work.

"Do you know if there's a girl here?" I ask. "She's new."

"Oh, the Pryce girl?" he inquires.

"Yeah, Lacey Pryce."

"She's here alright. Valentine has her protected like gold. I guess she is important."

Well, the good news is Lacey is here. The bad news is it sounds near impossible to get to her.

"All done. Well, Brock Anderson, it was a pleasure meeting you."

"Same to you Doc. Thank you again."

He nods and leaves.

Not even a minute later, Mike comes into the room. "Get up," he practically shouts. "You're going to take a shower, get some new clothes, and join Valentine for a meal."

A meal? This keeps getting weirder. "Will you tell him I don't kiss on the first date?'

"Shut up and follow me."

He escorts me to the showers where my bindings are removed. He has three others with him with their guns drawn.

"You guys going to watch me soap up or something?"

Mike's face turns red. "You're not funny. Make it quick."

The warm water feels like a massage. My body is caked with filth, my muscles ache, and I have more bruises than I care for. I use extra caution with my head. As the water falls, a mixture of black and brown slides into the drain. I get out and grab the new clothes prepared for me. The pair of jeans are almost identical to what I normally wear. The shirt left for me is Valentine's blue. It feels weird wearing his colors.

Mike and his henchmen escort me through Valentine's headquarters. We walk down a hallway similar to the conference area in our Hub.

Mike opens a door and points. "Take a seat."

Inside there is a round dining table with an elegant spread. Thick cloth napkins are creased in a perfect triangle with a spoon, fork, and knife. Two tall glasses of water each with a slice of lemon hanging off the side.

I take a seat. The chair feels like a feather filled pillow.

So many questions, no time to process.

The door opens, and Valentine walks in.

- Chapter 41 -

I almost laugh because Valentine is wearing the two-faced mask. I want to see his real face.

His lips move through the mouth hole. "There he is." That voice.

He's smiling even from inside the mask. "The man of the hour, Mr. Brock Anderson. God, you're difficult to get over here, you know that?"

"If I'd known I was supposed to be here, I would've made it easier." I'm unsettled.

"That's a good boy. But enough with the small chat, let's eat." Valentine signals to Mike to bring his chef in. "I hope you don't mind joining me for such a late meal. My business prevents me from keeping a normal schedule."

"Not at all." All of the running and combat depleted my energy reserves, and I feel the hunger.

The chef who walks in looks like a typical chef most people would picture, all white, greasy apron, muffin looking hat on top of his head. He carries a tray with two stainless steel dishes with lids covering the tops.

The chef places the dishes on our respective sides. When he raises the lid, the most savoring aroma wafts up to my nose. My saliva bursts like a waterfall. My stomach growls. The steam clears and there's a tender steak, fluffy white mashed potatoes with creamy brown gravy, a medley of vegetables, and a soft white roll with butter glazed over the top.

Valentine's voice breaks me from my food coma, "I assume you'll find this satisfying. Filet mignon, my favorite."

A warning flares in my mind. "Why're you doing this?"

Valentine holds his hands up. "Relax. No questions until you have enjoyed your meal."

There doesn't appear to be a threat he wants to poison me, unless he's one sick dude like Quentin, which I wouldn't put past him, but hell, if I'm going to die, might as well while eating the best meal of my life.

I dig into the food. I'm disappointed because I expect Valentine to take off his mask to eat, but he eats delicately, like a king, and doesn't get food stains on his mask.

Each bite of the steak is tender. The potatoes slide down my throat. The vegetables are the perfect blend of firm and soft. The roll melts in my mouth. I finish my last satisfying bite and relax back into my chair. I've never been so stuffed in my life.

"Suffice?" Valentine asks.

"Definitely."

"You had some questions?"

"How can you be so calm when there's a war happening outside?"

Valentine laughs, a real laugh. "Oh Brock, you know this is all just a game, don't you? This whole place is a joke of a way for the Acropolis to remain a safe haven."

His mocking tone boils my blood, with this game nonsense. It infuriates me to think my life is a set of puppet strings. "This is a game to you?" I seethe. "What the hell is wrong with you and Quentin? These are people's lives we're talking about. We're not playthings."

"You can be upset about the system, or you can think about the future."

"The future?"

"Here's the problem. The game is about to end. That's dangerous for us."

"What're you talking about?" Valentine almost speaks as much nonsense as Quentin.

"We'll get to that soon enough. First, I need to reveal something to you."

Valentine's right hand reaches for his mask. He slides it down. Both my hands brace on the chair. My gut told me, I didn't want to believe it.

I'm staring into the face of Vincent.

- Chapter 42 -

How can Vincent be here? He's outside fighting against Valentine's gang.

An amusing smile crosses over Vincent's face. "You look like you just saw a ghost." Gentle laughter follows his sarcastic comment.

My brain wracks through how this could be possible. Vincent's acted different the last few days. He sent a whiff of two personalities.

My eyes lower and look toward my hand, "Vincent, how do you do it?" I bring my fingers up and rub my eyes. This new information brings my mental exhaustion to the brink of a meltdown.

"It's complicated," is all he says.

My words spew. "Is this the reason why you weren't in the room during the Draft? This explains the mask, your double identity. But how? Does Quentin know? I looked up to you. You taught me everything."

It takes him a moment before he responds. "In due time. We cannot waste our energy on petty talk. We have larger issues at hand that need to be dealt with first."

Petty talk? I close my eyes again. This betrayal. It hurts. Vincent was always there, consistent. Consistency is not something one takes for granted in the Ashen Yard.

When I open my eyes again, Vincent's face is as still as stone, but nestled underneath there's a twinkle in his eye. He's entertained. Rage smolders within my core.

I pound my hands down on the table and stand up. "How could you do this?" The plates and silverware shake.

Vincent stands up, draws his gun, and points it in my face. "Don't push your luck." His cold gaze sends a shiver down my spine. "Sit your ass down!"

Mike barrels in through the door. "Is everything alright, Valentine?"

I laugh inside. Valentine. I cannot fathom the elaborate lie. It's inconceivably clever. I used to think Quentin was to the most feared in the Ashen Yard. I was wrong.

Vincent glares at Mike. "What the hell took you so long? If Brock had any sort of weapon, he'd be on top of me. You useless piece of..."

Mike looks like he's about to drop a load in his pants. Beads of sweat form upon his forehead. "I'm sorry, sir."

"Make yourself useful!" Vincent's voice rises. "Get our bargaining chip."

Mike salutes Vincent. "Yes, sir."

Vincent dismisses the gesture with the wave of his hand. Mike leaves, and Vincent returns his attention to me.

"I know what you want," he says.

"No kidding. You told me before I came here."

Vincent raises his hand up to his mouth, and it looks like he hiccups. "Of course. Why do you want her?"

"Well, I–" my voice stops. I wasn't prepared to answer that question.

"Ah yes, love," Vincent says. "Love does funny things to people."

I refuse to respond to his mocking tone.

He uses his finger to draw around the room. "You realize this is his fault, don't you? For you, me, your mother, and..."

I cut him off, "Whose fault? What're you talking about?"

"Your father's."

My world spins. How does my father bear the fault for me, my mother, and this psycho sitting across from me? This is the weirdest hour of my life, and considering what I've been through, that's saying something.

I gather my thoughts. "I don't follow. It's like you're speaking in some sort of code."

Vincent plays with something around his neck. I look closer and recognize the necklace. It has the same emblem from the one he gave me the night of my solo mission.

I pull mine out of my pocket and hold it up. "What sort of sick, twisted mind game are you playing?"

Vincent shudders for a moment, coughs, then laughs like I caught him off guard.

"Ah yes. There are so many dirty little secrets. You've been protected. This protection will leave you alone someday. I'm sad for you."

My patience falters, "Please talk like a normal person."

Before Vincent speaks again, Mike opens the door, and with him is Lacey. Her eyes shine when she sees me.

"Oh Brock," she musters and squeezes me tight. My bumps and bruises make me wince. She sniffles and her breath shakes.

"What a happy little reunion," says Vincent. "Time will tell if it's going to last."

Lacey pulls back with wet trails dribbling down both cheeks. I wrap my arm around her shoulder to ease her pain, our pain.

"You know what's happening here." Vincent points at Lacey. "You know about these men who're out to get us."

Lacey's eyes fall to the ground. Her feet wiggle back and forth.

"You're so valuable," Vincent continues. "Your father's running the operation. I'm sure he's worried about his little girl. How could he not keep you safe from being imprisoned?"

Vincent looks at me. "And it was because of you. This little love thing." A wicked grin a mile wide stretches the corners of his face.

"Me?" I reply.

"Oh my, how history repeats itself," says Vincent. "You're so much like your father. It disgusts me."

His dislike of my father is unsettling. A man who's a ghost, someone who I want forgotten is now haunting me, and I do not even know why.

Lacey squeezes me. "Don't listen to him. Everything was my choice."

Vincent's headquarters shake. Vincent shoots Mike a look. "Go see what's going on."

Mike leaves and is back within a few moments. "It's the gray men, sir. As you predicted, they're attacking."

Vincent raises his hands. "The time has come. It's our time. I'm going to prepare. You're to escort Brock and Lacey to the place. I will join you shortly."

- Chapter 43 -

Vincent splits off from the group, while Mike and the others herd Lacey and I along. Mike doesn't cuff us. This shows his confidence, or as I'd say, his stupidity. There's a chance for escape. I'll think of something soon.

I'm still recovering from shock learning the identity of Valentine, and from what I gather, no one else around here is aware.

Worry crosses Lacey's face. She's hiding something from me. An idea forms.

"Is there something you need to tell me?" I ask. "Why're you so important?"

She's lost for words. She really is hiding something.

"Quit with the chit chat and follow along," says Mike without turning his head.

"No!" I shout. This makes Lacey jump and her eyes open wide. "I want answers, now! I'm tired of secrets!"

I grab Lacey's shoulders and push her up against the wall. The act looks like it hurts more than it does. Despite my theatrics, I'm asking questions I want answers to. I read Lacey's emotional pain with a twist of guilt.

My actions grab the attention of our three escorts. One from behind grabs me and pulls back. I play along and act like the force makes me lose my balance, and we fall backwards.

Falling toward the opposite wall, I launch off my feet and my body crushes him. He grunts and the air burst from his lungs. I spin around, grab his gun, and hold him as a shield. My timing's right. Mike and his friend aim at me and shoot. The bullets hit their comrade. Pointing my gun at Mike, I connect with his shooting arm. The bullet rips right through his flesh. He yelps, drops his gun, and falls to the ground holding the gushing wound.

My attention shifts to my last target. The gun shakes in his hand. I shoot his thigh. He slides to the ground whimpering while holding his leg. To my surprise, Lacey punches him across the face.

"Nice," I say.

She grabs hold of a handgun off the ground and says, "We need to get out of here and find the Cleanse members."

"Cleanse members?" I'm completely confused.

"Sorry, we don't have time. Let's move."

"One second," I say.

Lacey looks at me with a sense of urgency. I walk over to Mike. He's still holding his arm, blood running down painting a red sleeve. He looks up like a scared animal. He reminds me of Tony so eager to please the big man.

I bend down, bringing my mouth to his ears and whisper, "You couldn't handle me when you had the advantage. You can take your cocky attitude and shove it up your ass." With a single punch, Mike's knocked out cold.

Lacey looks at me. "Sorry, he was so cocky and it bugged the hell out of me." I shrug my shoulders like I can't even convince myself.

Lacey responds, "If you're done now, let's get going."

"Hold on another second," I hold up my finger like I'm lecturing her. "I do want answers. We're surrounded by enemies. There's an enemy of my enemy attacking this compound."

Lacey holds up her hands. "No, no, no. The people who're here are not the enemy. We want to rendezvous with them, the Order of the Cleanse."

Vincent's voice booms from down the long hallway, "What the hell is going on?"

"Let's go," I tell Lacey.

I grab her arm and pull her. Bullets fly. I fire a few shots without much aim. Even though I don't connect with Vincent, it slows him down.

"Brock, you're making a foolish mistake," Vincent shouts.

I glance behind and see he stopped pursuing us. His handgun is at his side and a look of blind fury.

I don't allow my mind to think. I only command my body to run. We run past the room where I had my dinner date with Vincent. The fact the headquarters are basically identical makes it easy to navigate.

"Take a right at the next intersection," I say with a heavy breath. Lacey doesn't respond but keeps following.

We turn right. There's a door thirty feet around the corner. It should lead to the foyer where we can leave this place.

We push through the door and my instincts are correct. We stand atop the large staircase that looks down to the bottom floor, just like Quentin's. Men in gray stand at the bottom with their guns drawn. Some of Vincent's men are held hostage.

One looks up at us, points his gun, and yells, "Don't move!"

I stand still, but Lacey advances a bit further. "It's me."

Her voice draws everyone's attention. "Ms. Pryce, it's you." I follow the voice. It's Roy. "Thank god."

Roy and Lacey have been working together this whole time? That explains how easy it was to get into the Acropolis.

He ascends the stairs with a few of the other men. "Are you injured?"

"No, I am fine," Lacey responds. She looks toward me and sees my arms held up and two men pointing their guns at me. "He's with me. He saved my life."

"He's good," says Roy. "Come on, we must make haste."

We're escorted out of Vincent's headquarters. The men in gray holding their positions abandon their posts and follow the crowd.

Everyone runs at a brisk pace. I want to keep talking to Lacey, but it's impossible at the rate we travel. It's like she's escorted by her own personal guard. Roy keeps glancing at his watch.

We arrive at a familiar place. We're near the spot where I first encountered this group that mysterious night. The man in front of the group reaches for a bush, grabs the top, and pulls it over. An underground opening appears. One by one we file downward.

We enter an underground cavern that looks like something you would see in a spy movie. We walk down into a hallway made of metal beams mixed with compact dirt. Fluorescent lights line the tops of the cavern. We enter a large room. In the center of the room is a table that looks like something you'd see in a war room. Electrical wires strung along the walls connect computers and screens.

"We have her," Roy says. Everyone inside is relieved. "Please take her."

A couple of people jump from their seats and grab her.

Lacey tries to speak, "But..." She disappears into a different corridor.

"Who's this?" asks one of the men. "Did you guys get another one?"

Roy looks at me. "It's not confirmed, but I'm certain he's safe." Roy reaches into a pocket of his uniform and pulls out a scanner. He holds it up to my eyes and a small light reflects off them. After a second, he pulls it back and it glows green.

"Affirmative," says Roy with a grin on his face. "Brock

Anderson, you're a slippery one. Welcome to the Order of the Cleanse."

- Chapter 44 -

Before I can comprehend what's happening, I'm escorted from the big room. Food is offered, but my stomach is stuffed from Vincent's feast. I'm ordered to wait in a room.

The room is small, about eight by eight with a bed pushed up along the wall opposite of the door. While sitting on the edge of the bed, confusion and exhaustion cloud my head. Too much is going on. I strip down to my underwear and snuggle into bed. This recharge is necessary, too much information to process. As soon as my eyes close, sleep takes me away.

My mother's hurting. She lies on the ground with her hand outstretched. She's calling for me. She needs my help. I try to yell for her, but nothing escapes my mouth. I try again, still nothing. I run. Next, a sprint. The distance doesn't close. A silhouette looms over her. I yell again, nothing. The silhouette wraps around my mother and takes her into the darkness.

I shoot up. Sweat drips down my forehead. My breath's heavy like I was actually running. I gaze around the room, no changes. My clothes lie in the same spot. These Cleanse people think I should be happy I'm in their care, but really, I feel like a prisoner.

I swing off the bed and get back into my clothes. Walking over to the door, I'm about to pull down on the handle when it turns on its own. The door opens and Roy walks into the room.

"I apologize for how long it took for us to get back here," Roy says. "There's so much happening. We're trying to stay organized."

I shrug. "I caught some sleep."

"Quite good," he replies. "Ms. Pryce requested I show you around. She regrets not being here, but she's dealing with other matters. She hopes to see you soon."

I scratch the top of my head, "Alright. So, you're showing me around?"

"Ah, yes, sir. We are most grateful you brought Ms. Pryce back to us." Roy bows and heads out the door.

He motions for us to go down the hall. "I assume you have questions."

"Absolutely."

"This show and tell should answer most of them."

Roy guides me down the hallway. He turns and asks, "Where shall I begin?"

"My first question is, where are we?" I think about my question and rephrase. "Well, I know where we are, but what is this?"

Roy nods. "This is where the Order of the Cleanse operates." I'm about to ask another question, but Roy puts his finger up, "I already know your second question. The Order of the Cleanse are good people. They're working within a tight timeframe to get certain people to safety."

"What people?" I ask.

"Prisonborns. People like you."

"But why?"

"We'll come to that in a second." Roy leads the way standing with his chest out.

Down the hallway, we pass doorways, some open, some closed, and people here and there. Each person we pass highly regards Roy. They stop and salute with respect. Roy returns the salutes without pausing his pace.

We come to the large room with the huge center table and computers lined up along the walls. People pack the room doing different jobs, some looking at the monitors, others deep in conversation.

"This is the Strategy Room," Roy says. "This is where the Order of the Cleanse carries out its operation to gather as many Prisonborns before the Cleanse."

"What is this Cleanse?" I ask.

"The government is shutting down the Ashen Yard prisons all over the country. They plan to Cleanse each prison by extermination. They want a fresh start, like pushing a reset button."

I cut in, "And you're gathering Prisonborns because?"

Roy finishes the thought, "Because we're sympathizers for anyone who is unjustly imprisoned. The government knew families developed in the prison and did little to change the system. The government wanted to begin the Cleanse, but the Order petitioned with a plan to gather Prisonborns. We were given a time window, and that window is closing."

"Is that why everyone expects me to be thankful?" My voice is steady but throws some heat. I'm not going to kiss the toes of anyone who thinks they're high and mighty.

"Well, the Order is doing this for people like you," Roy says.

"And people like my mother, right?"

"If she's Prisonborn, then yes. What is her name?"

"Laura Mae Anderson."

Roy stops to think for a moment. "That name doesn't sound familiar, but we received some more Prisonborns. We'll go there shortly."

Roy stops at the large table. I look at the top surface. It's a map of the Ashen Yard with standing figures positioned around the map.

Roy points. "This is where we strategize to rescue you

Prisonborns."

The phrase 'you Prisonborns' sounds condescending. Roy keeps speaking, but I don't hear the words. I analyze how he presents himself. Every word he speaks comes out with a hint of a smile. He's proud. This rubs me wrong. I'm not sure if this is the reaction I should have. I mean, they did rescue me. My thoughts flood to my mother. I pray she's alright. Hopefully nothing happened to her during the war.

My thoughts scatter and Roy's voice reaches my ears. "The Order planned small attacks to track patterns of our documented Prisonborns. We would study, attack again, and set ourselves in favorable positions. We'd gather who we could, when we could."

I remember the first night I saw the Order. I saw them scan the eyes of a prisoner like they did to me when I got here, and I watched them shoot the prisoner who was still alive.

"What about the non-Prisonborns?" I ask.

Roy almost laughs and waves his hands. "They aren't in our directive, nor a priority for anyone. We deal with them when necessary."

He says it so matter-of-factly like non-Prisonborns are expendable resources. My fall from grace is far greater than many inside the Ashen Yard. I guess my condemned birth makes me better.

Roy's voice brings me back. "Let's check on our new Prisonborns. Maybe you'll see your mother."

The thought of seeing my mother takes me out of my somber mood. Roy takes me through another hallway connected to the Strategy Room.

There's a man with a clipboard standing outside a doorway. Roy looks at him, "Kent with the clipboard. Let me see the report." He hands over the clipboard, and Roy reads the print.

"Is this all?" Roy asks.

Kent adjusts his glasses. “Actually, there’s one more in quarantine. She’s being monitored.”

I nearly jump, “Is it my mother?”

“Would you like me to take you?” he asks.

“Please.”

We head down another hallway and enter a room with a large glass window connected to another room. Inside, my mother lays on a gurney hooked up to machines.

- Chapter 45 -

I run to the window and shout for her.

"She can't hear you," Roy says from behind me. "This is like an interrogation room. She can only hear you when you push this button and talk into the microphone."

I run over to the microphone, push the button, and speak without permission. "Mom, mom, can you hear me?"

She stirs at the sound of my voice and looks a groggy. "Brock?" Her voice sounds like a frog.

"It's me." Tears fall down my face. I turn toward Roy and Kent. "Let me inside!"

Kent shakes his head. "I'm sorry, she's under..."

I interrupt, "I don't care. You will let me in!" I'm desperate enough I'll do something rash.

Roy nudges Kent. "Let him in."

Roy nods and uses he badge to scan the door. It opens, and I rush inside.

I grab her hand not connected to an IV. "I'm here." I inventory her body for injuries. She appears unscathed on the outside. Her hands squeeze mine. Her face is full of color. She looks tired.

"I'm glad you're safe," her voice croaks. "I was so worried."

"No more worrying. We're in the care of these people

here."

She sighs and smiles.

A door in the back opens and in steps three people dressed in scrubs. They grab my mother's gurney. "We need her," one of them says.

I step forward to protest but a hand pulls me back. It's Roy. "We should let them do their job."

I breathe in. "You're right." My mind goes to my mother's medical condition. Maybe this Order can cure her.

Roy speaks through my thoughts, "I was informed we have a meeting."

"With."

"Follow me to see the leader of this operation."

- Chapter 46 -

I follow Roy like a robot oblivious to my surroundings. We approach a door that's larger than the others. Two men with guns stand post. Warning sirens blare in my head. The guards salute Roy. The door opens and Roy steps inside. I stay back, but he turns and beckons me to follow.

We enter an elaborate room. It reminds me of a room described in large mansions, apart from the low ceiling. There's a large desk with an enormous leather chair with its back facing us. Maps are posted on the walls. Bookshelves line most of the perimeter.

Lacey stands behind one corner of the desk. My heart skips until I see tears running down her cheeks.

That's when something on the desk captures my attention. Something so familiar. I focus and see one of my drawings. The one I sold to...

As if on cue, the leather chair swivels around and there sits Mr. P. I'm stunned. The connection clicks. Mr. P is Mr. Pryce.

"Lieutenant Roy reporting." He stands tall with a crisp salute.

"At ease," says Mr. P. He looks at Lacey, "It's because of him?"

"What do you mean, Mr. P?" I ask.

He snaps, "Enough!" He pauses. "Enough," less intense. "The name is Mr. Pryce. Your little fling with my daughter almost got her killed!" He approaches me with his finger pointing into my chest. This interaction with him is a far different experience than the Forum.

"Daddy," Lacey cries. "It's not his fault."

Mr. Pryce moves away from me and relaxes. "Yes, you made that quite clear. But I'm still furious."

"Don't be mad at Brock, be mad at me," she sniffles when she says it.

"You're damn right I'm pissed at you, but I'm pissed at him too."

I intervene in the fiery words. "What's going on?"

He turns toward me, "My daughter has a criminal record because of you." He points at Lacey. "That was a damn good job you lost." He turns back to me. "Thank goodness you're Prisonborn, because..." the thought fizzles.

Again, with this righteousness of the people down here. I state the positive. "No offense sir, but she's healthy and standing next to you."

His face softens. He stands up and hugs Lacey, squeezes her in, and whispers something into her ear. She nods.

"Thank you, Brock," he says. "I got caught up in my emotions. I thought I was going to lose my baby girl."

He gives her a half hug and returns to his chair. He looks at the drawing I sold him. "Fate is weird. Who would've thought how connected we would become?"

I huff, "Yeah, it's weird."

Mr. Pryce points between Lacey and me. "This little fling is going to stop." Lacey tries to interject, but he denies her words. "Don't push it. I haven't gone through Hell to get lip service from you."

Hell, I think. He has no idea.

Mr. Pryce clears his throat. "Please escort our guest back to his quarters and report back for our briefing," he says to

Roy.

Roy crisply salutes. “Sir.”

He escorts me back to the small room, exchanges pleasantries, and leaves me inside.

While in the room, I recount the crazy past twenty four hours. I count my blessings. I’m safe while my mother and Lacey are both here. This situation feels safer than if the three of us were in the Ashen Yard.

A gentle knock interrupts my thoughts. The door opens and Lacey walks in. Her eyes light up and she kisses me before I can react.

I hold back. “Are you not going to listen to your father? He’s scary.”

Lacey laughs. “He’s running on raw emotion. I mean, he thought he lost his only daughter.”

She moves in and kisses me again.

“Oh, I almost forgot,” she says and pulls a bag off her back. “This is for you.”

I open the bag and see a notebook, pencils, and those delicious chocolate cakes she introduced me to in the Acropolis.

“I figured you might get bored and want to draw. And I hope the cakes cheer you up and help celebrate our good fortune,” she says with a smile.

“I love it.” I falter for a moment. “Do you know what’s going on with my mother?”

Lacey softens. “I heard they are taking care of her. Everything will be fine. I’ll bug the people watching over her. I promise I’ll report the good news to you as soon as I find out.”

I let out a breath. “Thank you.”

“I better get going. My father still needs to cool down. I promise he will warm up to you. To us.” She kisses me again. “Get some well-deserved rest.”

“Is that an order?”

She salutes, "Absolutely." She hugs me and leaves the room.

I crawl into bed and relax. I close my eyes and cannot help but smile. I thought Lacey was an impossible dream. Turns out she's not. Everyone I care about is here. For the first time in my life, I can be safe and comfortable. I gladly give in to the notion and fall into a deep sleep.

Jeff Spaur

Jeff Spaur makes his writing debut with The Ashen Yard. He lives in Richland, Washington with his wife and two sons. He wants to continue creating stories for readers to enjoy.

Find him on:

FaceBook, Twitter, Instagram: @spaurhawk

TikTok: @spaurhawk1034